Computer Classics ®

™

Rebecca

Edward Ronny Arnold

Computer Classics ®
NASHVILLE

רבקה

Published by
Computer Classics ®
497 Elysian Fields Road A-11
Nashville, Tennessee 37211

Rebecca © is published in e-book format by **Computer Classics** ® on the **Computer Classics** ® website www.computer-classics.com.

Rebecca © paperback published in June 2002

Computer Classics ® is a registered Federal Trademark

The Hebrew letters רבקה ™ which form the name Rebecca is a registered State Trademark.

Library of Congress Control Number: 2002092367
ISBN: 0-9721216-1-7

Printed in the United States of America

רבקה

Contents

Rebecca 9

　Prologue to Rebecca 9

　Scroll I 13

　Scroll II 15

　Scroll III 17

　Scroll IV 21

　Scroll V 23

　Scroll VI 25

　Scroll VII 27

　Scroll VIII 31

　Scroll IX 39

Rebecca II 41

　Prologue to Rebecca II 41

　Rebecca II 43

　The Soldiers are Baptized unto Christ 46

　The Gift is Passed to Another 49

　Aaron Passes the Gift to Another 50

　The Passing of Justin 51

Epilogue to Rebecca II 53

　1945 53

　1980 55

　2001 - A Small City in the American Midwest 57

6

רבקה
Contents

The Ten Scrolls 59

    The Command of Pilate 59

    The Soldiers Come to Titus 59

    The Plan of Titus 61

    Pilate Burns the Tenth Scroll 63

The Deliverance of Evan 65

    Prologue - The Deliverance of Evan 65

    Jacob Battles to Free Rebecca 67

    Elizabeth Healed by God 71

    The Angel of God Delivers Evan 72

    God Heals Jacob 75

    The Journey Home 75

The Plot of Satan 77

    God Heals Rebecca 77

    The Plot of the Three Serpents 78

    Satan Lures the Child to Stone 79

    Three Serpents Consumed by the Fire of God 79

    The Plot of the Beast 80

    The Beast Consumed by the Fire of God 81

    The Command of Satan 83

    The Spirit of Jaykal Brought Unto the Kingdom of God 84

Jerron 85

    Jerron 85

רבקה

Contents

The Gift of Food and Cloth 85

The Gift of Copper, Silver, and Gold 87

The Greatest Gift 88

God Heals Jerron 88

Jerron Draws Water 90

Jerron Plows the Field 91

The Angel of God Delivers Jest 92

Many Work as One 95

Jerron Speaks the Law 96

The Eleven Gather Together 96

The Freed Servants Leave Jerron 97

The Search for Evan and Jacob 97

God Delivers Hebron 99

The Many Work As One 99

The Harvest is Divided 99

Jacob Battles the Soldiers 102

The Thirteen Protect the People 106

The Plot of the Tax Collector 107

The Angel of God Delivers the Thirteen 108

The Angel of God Delivers Hebron 109

Hebron is at Peace 110

The Judging of Nafta, Brema, and Salan 113

Prologue to The Judging of Nafta, Brema, and Salan 113

8

רבקה

Contents

The Judging of Nafta, Brema, and Salan 115

Beathag 121

Tamiko 129

The Child of the People 133

Six Years Later 139

Timothy 159

Epilogue to Timothy 166

Elizabeth 169

Ebet 183

Rachel's Secret 199

The Search for Rachel 199

Rachel Reveals Her Secret 205

God Heals Laurie 210

The Gift is Passed to Another 211

Appendix 213

The Children 213

The Author 221

רבקה
Rebecca
Prologue to Rebecca

In 1932, an archeological dig near the city of Jerusalem uncovered a mass grave. Within the grave the skeletal remains of men, women, and children were found.

The mass grave contained three mysteries.

The first mystery is the grave contained the skeletal remains of thirty-six Roman soldiers. The soldiers were identified by their armor.

The second mystery is among the skeletal remains was an earthen jar. The earthen jar contained the charred ash of several scrolls.

The third mystery is among the skeletal remains of men, women, and children were the skeletal remains of one horse.

The horse was the property of a soldier of high rank. The saddle was engraved with the seal of Caesar.

The remains were dated to the time of Christ.

In 37 CE, Tiberius summoned Pontius Pilate to Rome. Scholars believe Tiberius summoned Pilate because Tiberius learned Pilate executed several soldiers without trial. The soldiers were reported to have defied Pilate's command and Pilate had them burned alive at Gehenna.

At the time Pilate was summoned to Rome, Tiberius gathered together the fiercest of his soldiers. The soldiers were chosen from all of his legions and the legion contained more than three thousand soldiers.

The soldiers were sent to Galilee to the city of Cana.

There were several unusual things about this legion.

The soldiers who formed the legion were picked from other legions. The legion had no name or seal.

The legion did not have horses. The legion contained no cavalry. All of the soldiers were foot soldiers. The commanders did not ride horses.

It was the custom of Caesar for soldiers to beat drums, blow trumpets, and wave the banner of Caesar when the soldiers were ordered to attack. The legion did not include soldiers who carried drums, trumpets, or the banner of Caesar.

The soldiers wore heavy armor. Only the largest and strongest of the soldiers could wear the armor. One commander wrote of this legion, "This is the greatest army ever to walk on earth."

One of the most unusual things about this legion is that no one knows why the army was sent to Cana. There was no rebellion in Cana and no army threatened Galilee.

The city of Cana is known for one thing. The apostle Simon Peter preached the gospel of Christ at Cana. Cana is located south of Jotapata and north of Sepphoris.

However, the most unusual thing about this legion sent to Cana by Tiberius is that the legion never returned. The legion traveled by ships to the port of Ptolemais. And from the port of Ptolemais, the legion marched to Cana. It is not known if the legion reached Cana for no soldier returned.

At the time the soldiers marched to Cana, Tiberius died. The death of Tiberius is shrouded in mystery.

At the time Tiberius died, Pilate died. Scholars believe Pilate committed suicide.

Caligula replaced Tiberius.

The ships, used by the legion sent to Cana, remained at the port of Ptolemais for many months. The ships were unmanned.

Caligula sent soldiers to retrieve the ships and the ships were returned to a port near Rome.

There is no written record of why the legion was sent to Cana and there is no written record of why the legion did not return.

Gehenna is a valley near the city of Jerusalem. Gehenna is where the trash of Jerusalem was gathered and burned. An archeological dig at the site of Gehenna, in 1951, uncovered the charred skeletal remains of six men. Five of the six men were soldiers. Nothing is known of the sixth man. Near the sixth man was a large earthen jar. The earthen jar contained nine scrolls written by a man named Titus. Fires did not damage the scrolls.

The identify of Titus is not known.

One scholar believes Titus was a scribe to Pontius Pilate and Herod Antipas. The scrolls were dated to the time of Christ.

The scrolls were written in Latin. Below are the words of the scroll, translated into English, as written by Titus. The scrolls tell the story of Rebecca and the scrolls are titled Rebecca.

רבקה

רבקה
Scroll I
Rebecca

Our Savior and Lord Jesus Christ had been crucified, buried, and raised. And the risen Christ had sent his disciples to spread the word that he had been raised.

And the disciples spread the word of the risen Christ. And the disciples performed miracles of healing.

And one of these disciples was named Simon Peter. And Simon Peter performed miracles of healing in the town of Jerusalem.

And word came that a great healer was in Jerusalem. And the great healer had healed all who were sick and infirmed. And the great healer had made blind men to see and cripples to walk. And the great healer was to leave the city.

And many traveled to Jerusalem to see the great healer and to be healed by him. And the lepers came to the city. And the lepers were driven from the city for the lepers were the unclean of the unclean.

And the lepers waited at the gates of the city for the great healer to pass. And as they waited their numbers increased.

And the great healer came to the gates of the city. And the road was filled of the sick and the infirmed. And as the great healer passed, all within his reach were healed. And those not near to touch the great healer reached for his shadow. And those who touched the shadow of the great healer were healed.

And the lepers went to the road and the crowd drove them back. For the lepers were the unclean of the unclean. Three times the lepers went to the road and three times they were driven back.

And the crowd cheered for they were healed. And the lepers wept for they were not healed.

And the great healer passed on the road and he heard the cry of a young child. And the great healer stopped and commanded all to be silent. And all were silent. And the only sound was the cry of a young child.

And the great healer left the road and went to where the child lay. And the great healer stood before the child. And the child was a leper and a cripple. And the great healer stood among the lepers.

And the great healer took the child and held up the child for all to see and he spoke to the crowd saying, "All are worthy of God's grace. Not one man, one woman, one child, or one of the unclean of the unclean is unworthy."

And the great healer whispered in the ear of the child and the child's cries stopped.

And again the great healer held up the child for all to see and again he spoke to the crowd saying, "The power of God has healed this child."

And the great healer passed his hand over the child and a third time he held up the child for all to see. And a third time he spoke to the crowd saying, "It is the will of God that for generations to come all with know the power of God through the hands of a child. What was given to me has been given to her. This child is protected by God himself. No man, woman, child, or beast of the earth shall harm this child. This is the will of God."

And the great healer handed the child to her parents and he touched them and he blessed them. And he spoke to them saying, "Your child will serve God. Return to your place and share the blessing which God has given."

And the great healer did not return to the road. The great healer walked among the lepers. And as he walked among them he touched them. He touched them all. And as he touched them they were healed. All were healed

And the great healer returned to the road. And the crowd cheered for all had been healed.

And the child was returned to her place. And people came to the place of the child to see the child healed by God and blessed by God.

And the sick and the infirmed came to the place of the child. And they touched the child and the child touched them. And God healed all who touched the child and were touched by the child.

רבקה

Scroll II
The Fire of God Consumes Three Serpents

And the child wandered from her place to a place of stone.

And among the stone three serpents lay.

And when the child neared the stone the three serpents came to the child. And the three serpents went before and after the child.

And Josep missing the child called to the child. And hearing not the child, Josep searched for the child.

And Josep found the child near stone. And three serpents went before and after the child.

And Josep called for the child. And the child came to Josep. And the three serpents barred the path.

And the three serpents moved around the child. And the three serpents whipped their tails at the child. And the three serpents barred their fangs to the child.

And the child being young of age knew not the danger of the three serpents. And the child cried not.

And the three serpents neared the child. And the first of the three struck at the child. And the first of the three became as of fire. And the fire consumed the serpent.

And the second and third of the three struck at the child. And the second and third of the three became as of fire. And the fire consumed the serpents.

And Josep held the child and spoke to the child saying, "God himself protected you. For the three serpents were consumed in fire. And only the fire of God could consume the three serpents before they struck."

רבקה

Scroll III
The Healing of Cephus and Jerron

And word of the child came to Cephus. And Cephus was of God and a follower of the Christ. And Cephus fell ill. And Cephus being too ill to travel to the child sent several to the place of the child.

And the several asked of Josep and Mira that the child be brought to Cephus. For Cephus was too ill to travel.

And Josep, Mira, the child, and the several traveled to Hebron to the place of Cephus. For Cephus was of God and a follower of the Christ.

And Cephus lay on cloth. And the body of Cephus bears the marks of sores. And Cephus was near death.

And Cephus spoke to Josep, Mira, and the child saying, "Word of the child healed by God and blessed by God has reached my ear. If it is the will of God, God will heal me through the hands of the child. If it is the will of God that I will not be healed, the child will touch me not."

And Cephus asked of Josep and Mira that the child may come near. And Cephus held out his hand to the child and he touched the child. And the child touched the hand of Cephus.

And Cephus was healed by the power of God through the hands of the child.

And many came to the place of Cephus to see the child healed by God and blessed by God. And the ill and the infirmed came to the place of Cephus. And they touched the child and the child touched them. And God healed all who touched the child and were touched by the child.

And servants brought Jerron to the place of Cephus. And Jerron was wealthy and commanded many servants. And the servants lay Jerron near the child. And Jerron touched the child and the child did not touch Jerron.

For Jerron was not of God or a follower of the Christ. And Jerron cared not for those of misfortune. And Jerron was not healed.

And the servants returned Jerron to his place.

And the servants of Jerron brought gifts for Josep, Mira, and the child. And the servants lay before them gifts of cloth and food. And the gifts were given to those of misfortune.

And the servants brought Jerron to the place of Cephus. And the servants lay Jerron near the child. And Jerron touched the child and the child did not touch Jerron.

For Jerron was not of God or a follower of the Christ. And Jerron cared not for those of misfortune. And Jerron was not healed.

And the servants returned Jerron to his place

And the servants of Jerron brought gifts for Josep, Mira, and the child. And the servants lay before them gifts of copper, silver, and gold. And the gifts were given to those of misfortune.

And the servants brought Jerron to the place of Cephus. And the servants lay Jerron near the child. And Jerron touched the child and the child did not touch Jerron.

For Jerron was not of God or a follower of the Christ. And Jerron cared not for those of misfortune. And Jerron was not healed.

And the servants returned Jerron to his place.

And Jerron called forth his servants. And he spoke to them saying, "My wealth is but metal and soil. And I fear the thief who will take my metal and soil. The wealth of God knows no limit and no thief can steal that which God gives. Three times I touched the child and three times the child touched me not. Two times I sent gifts to the child and two times the gifts were given to those of misfortune."

"God knows my heart. And my heart is not of God. I am not a follower of the Christ for I care not for those of misfortune."

And Jerron freed his servants. And he divided his wealth among them. And Jerron sent cloth, food, and coin to those of misfortune.

And Jerron prayed to God to enter his heart.

And the freed servants brought Jerron to the place of Cephus. And the freed servants lay Jerron near the child.

And Jerron spoke to Josep, Mira, and the child saying, "God has entered my heart. My wealth was of man. I seek the wealth of God. For the wealth of man is but metal and soil. The wealth of God is through his promise of eternal life through the teachings of the Christ. For all that believe in the Christ and follow the Christ will enter the kingdom of God. Though I die, I live."

And the child went to the bed of Jerron. And the child lay in the arms of Jerron.

And God healed Jerron through the hands of the child. For God knew the heart of Jerron. And Jerron was of God and a follower of the Christ.

Scroll IV
The Beast Consumed by the Fire of God

God healed Cephus through the hands of the child as he was of God and a follower of the Christ. And the family and the child stayed at the place of Cephus for many days.

And the family and the child were to return to their place.

And Cephus stopped them and spoke to them saying, "A beast roams the hill and this beast has killed cattle and man. Take these three men and they will protect your journey home."

And the three men were armed with spear, sword, and shield. And Cephus charged them to guard and protect Josep, Mira, and the child. And one went before and two went after.

And they approached a place of wood and stone and the beast charged the one who went before and struck him down. And the two who went after charged the beast with spear and sword. And they struck the beast with spear and sword and the beast was not harmed. And the beast struck down the two who went after.

And Josep, Mira, and the child stood before the beast.

And the child being young of age knew not the danger of the beast. And the child cried not.

And the beast roared. And the beast pawed the ground. And the beast bared its teeth.

And the beast charged the child. And the beast neared the child and the beast became as of fire. And the fire consumed the beast.

And the one who went before was dead from the beast and the two who went after were harmed.

And God healed the two who went after through the hands of the child.

And Josep, Mira, the child, and the two who went after returned to the place of the child. And the two who went after bore the one who went before. And the two who went after spoke of the beast that killed their brethren and the beast not harmed by sword or spear. And the fire of God consumed the beast. For the child was protected by God himself. No man, woman, child, or beast of the earth shall harm the child.

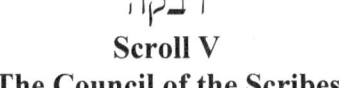

Scroll V
The Council of the Scribes

And word of the beast reached the ear of Pilate and Pilate called together his soldiers and scribes.

And Pilate commanded of them of the child. And the scribes said, "The child was a leper and a cripple. The child was healed by God and given the gift to heal. For generations to come all will know the power of God through the hands of a child. And God himself protects the child. No man, woman, child, or beast of the earth shall harm the child."

"And the fire of God has consumed three serpents that sought to harm the child and the fire of God has consumed the beast that killed one and struck down two."

And Pilate commanded of them, "Is this child the Christ?"

And the scribes responded, "This child is not the Christ. The Christ was the Son of God. And the Christ was crucified, died, and raised from the dead. The Christ is now with God."

"The child has performed no miracle save healing the sick."

And Pilate commanded of them, "Is this God the same God who allowed the Christ to be crucified among thieves?"

And the scribes answered, "Surely this is the same God. For the God of the Christ rose his son from the dead and only the God of the Christ could destroy the beast."

And Braka, a soldier of Pilate, mocked the scribes saying, "What God would allow his son to die among thieves?"

And the scribes responded saying, "Christ died for the sins of all that all may inherit God's kingdom. This child is not the Christ. This child has been given the power to heal that all generations will know God's power through the hands of a child."

And Braka asked of Pilate, "I will take the child and bring the child before Pilate that Pilate may witness this power of healing?"

רבקה

And Pilate commanded of Braka saying, "If this child is protected by a God, I will see you no more. If these stories are false, I will witness for myself if this child has the power to heal."

And Braka responded to Pilate saying, "If this child has the power of life the child has the power of death."

And the scribes responded saying, "This child does not have the power of life for the one that went before was killed by the beast and he lies dead. Only the Christ had the power of life. The child has the power to heal and not of life or death."

And Braka asked of Pilate, "If this child has the power to heal surely this child has the power of death. This child must be destroyed lest the child murder us all?"

And Pilate commanded of Braka, "Do as you will."

And Braka left the council to murder the child. And he took with him seven and twenty.

רבקה

Scroll VI
Braka Consumed by the Fire of God

And Braka and the seven and twenty went to seek the child. And many followed after them.

And Braka came to the place of the child and commanded that the child be brought to him.

And the two who went after were not at the place of the child for they mourned the death of the one who went before. And the child was without guard.

And Josep, Mira, and the child came from their place and stood before Braka.

And Josep asked, "Why do you want the child?"

And Braka spoke saying, "This child has offended Pilate. Give her to me that I may take her to him."

And Josep responded, "The child has done no harm to the prefect."

And Braka commanded saying, "The child is to be brought to Pilate that he may judge the child."

And Josep responded saying, "Only God will judge this child. For this child serves only God."

And the words of Josep angered Braka. And Braka drew his sword saying, "This child shall die!"

And Braka drew his sword. And the sword became as of fire and the fire consumed him.

And the seven and twenty seeing this drew their swords and ran to the child. And when the seven and twenty neared the child, their swords became as of fire and the fire consumed them.

And the crowd that followed moved backward for they had seen the fire of God. And one man took a stone that he may stone the child. And when the man raised the stone, the stone became as of fire and the fire consumed him.

And the man was one of many but no other was consumed. For only the man sought to harm the child and only the man was consumed.

And the crowd ran for God had protected the child. And the fire of God consumed Braka, the seven and twenty, and the man with stone.

And Joseph and Mira took the child and fled the city. And the two who went after fled with them for they had been charged by Cephus to guard and protect the child.

And they sought the apostle Simon Peter that he may give his council. For the child was protected by God himself and neither beast nor man had harmed the child. For the unseen hand of God consumed them in fire.

Scroll VII
The Guard of Pilate Consumed by the Fire of God

And word of this event came to the centurion of Pilate's guard and he assembled the guard.

And the soldiers of horse numbered thirty and the soldiers of foot numbered one hundred and ten. And the soldiers who bear the drum numbered twelve and the soldiers who bear the horn numbered twelve and the soldiers who bear the standard of Caesar numbered twelve.

And the centurion commanded the soldiers of horse to find the child and hold the child.

And the soldiers of foot followed.

And the soldiers of horse found Josep, Mira, the child, and the two who went after outside the city. And the soldiers of horse barred the path.

And the centurion assembled the soldiers of foot and the soldiers of foot surrounded the child.

And the soldiers of horse barred the north. And the soldiers of foot barred the east, south, and west.

And Josep, Mira, the child, and the two who went after stood in the middle.

And the centurion assembled the soldiers who bear the drum, the horn, and the standard of Caesar on a rise of sand.

And the centurion rode before the soldiers who bear the drum and commanded of his soldiers saying, "Your brethren are no more. A God protects the child and this god destroyed your brethren. We will avenge their death by murdering the child and all who stand with her. The soldiers of Rome fear not man or God. The soldiers of Rome fear only Caesar. Caesar gives us life. Caesar gives us death. We live only to serve Caesar."

And the centurion drew his sword and the soldiers of horse held up their spears and the soldiers of foot drew their swords.

And the centurion commanded of his soldiers saying, "The desert sand thirsts for the blood of the child and all who stand with her. The sand shall drink of their blood for man and God fall before the soldiers of Caesar."

And the centurion commanded the soldiers who bear the drum to beat the drum. And the soldiers beat the drum.

And the centurion commanded the soldiers who bear the horn to blow the horn. And the soldiers blew the horn.

And the centurion commanded the soldiers who bear the standard of Caesar to unfurl the banner of Caesar. And the soldiers unfurled the banner of Caesar.

And the centurion commanded the soldiers of foot to beat their swords against their shield. And the soldiers beat their swords against their shield.

And the centurion road before the soldiers who bear the standard and banner of Caesar and the centurion commanded the soldiers to sound the yell of war. And the soldiers sounded the yell of war.

And Josep, Mira, the child, and the two who went after stood in the middle. And the two who went after held their shields and drew their swords for battle.

And they stood amongst the soldiers of horse that numbered thirty and the soldiers of foot that numbered one hundred and ten. And the soldiers who bear the drum and the horn and the standard and banner of Caesar numbered thirty and six. And the centurion who commanded the soldiers numbered one.

And the child being young of age knew not the danger. And the child cried not.

And the centurion rode before the soldiers who bear the standard and banner of Caesar. And the centurion commanded the soldiers to attack.

And the soldiers of horse charged with spear and shield. And the soldiers of foot charged with sword and shield.

And the two who went after stood before the child with sword and shield.

And the soldiers of horse neared the child and their spears became as of fire. And the fire consumed soldier and horse.

And the soldiers of foot neared the child and their swords became as of fire. And the fire consumed them.

And the sword of the centurion that rode before the soldiers that bear the standard and banner of Caesar became as of fire. And the fire consumed the centurion.

And the fire did not consume the horse of the centurion for the horse sought not to harm the child.

And the fire did not consume the soldiers that bear the drum for the soldiers sought not to harm the child.

And the fire did not consume the soldiers who bear the horn for the soldiers sought not to harm the child.

And the fire did not consume the soldiers who bear the standard and the banner of Caesar for the soldiers sought not to harm the child.

And the soldiers not consumed numbered thirty and six. And the horse not consumed numbered one. For all who sought to harm the child were consumed by the fire of God. The fire of God consumed beast and man.

For as spoken by the apostle Simon Peter,' This child is protected by God himself. No man, woman, child, or beast of the earth shall harm this child."

And the soldiers who bear the drum released the drum and fled to the city.

And the soldiers who bear the horn released the horn and fled to the city.

And the soldiers who bear the standard and the banner of Caesar released the standard and the banner of Caesar and fled to the city.

And the horse not consumed followed the soldiers.

And Josep, Mira, the child, and the two who went after fled to the city of Nazareth to seek the apostle Simon Peter.

Scroll VIII
The Council of Pilate

And word of these events was sent to Pilate and Pilate summoned his soldiers and scribes.

And Pilate asked of them, "What harm has come to Braka?"

And the Scribe said, "Braka sought to murder the child and the unseen hand of God consumed him with fire. And the seven and the twenty sought to murder the child and the fire of God consumed them. And one man sought to murder the child with stone and the fire of God consumed him. And the man was of many and only he was consumed."

"And the child was taken from the city."

And Pilate asked of them, "What harm has come to my guard?"

And the scribe said, "The centurion of Pilate's guard sent the soldiers of horse to bar the path of the child. And the soldiers of foot followed."

"And the soldiers of horse numbered thirty and they sought to murder the child and they were consumed by the fire of God. And the soldiers of foot numbered one hundred and ten and they sought to murder the child and the fire of God consumed them. And the centurion who ordered the soldiers to murder the child numbered one and the fire of God consumed the centurion. And the soldiers who bear the drum and the horn and the standard and banner of Caesar numbered thirty and six were not consumed for they sought not to harm the child. And the horse of the centurion was not consumed for the horse sought not to harm the child."

"All who sought to harm the child, beast or man, were consumed by the fire of God."

And Pilate asked, "Is this the God of Moses and the Christ? For the God of Moses destroyed the army of Pharaoh and the God of the Christ raised him from the dead."

And the scribe spoke saying, "Surely, this is the same God."

And a soldier of Pilate asked, "I will take the army to destroy the child?"

And the scribe spoke, "God protects the child. All who sought to harm the child were consumed in fire. The serpents, beast, Braka, the seven and twenty, and the one man who sought to stone the child died at the unseen hand of God."

"The God who destroyed Braka, the seven and twenty, and the man with stone destroyed the guard of Pilate. Thirty and four beasts of the earth sought to harm the child. And the fire of God destroyed the beasts. One hundred and forty nine men sought to harm the child. And the fire of God destroyed the men."

And the solider asked, "We must inform Caesar?"

And the scribe responded, "Caesar must never know of these events. For if Caesar has knowledge of these events, he would surely send the legions of Rome to seek the child to murder the child. And this God would destroy the legions of Rome, nay, this God would destroy Caesar himself for Caesar would order the child's death."

And Pilate responded, "Why am I living? Did I not order the death of the child at the hands of Braka?"

And the scribe responded, "Pilate did not order the death of the child. Pilate did not seek to harm the child. Braka sought to bring the child to Pilate for judgment. Pilate told Braka, 'If a God protects the child, I will see you no more." Pilate did not seek to harm the child but surely Caesar would order the child's death. And at the first strike against the child God would destroy soldier and Caesar. The centurion of the guard was destroyed for he ordered the child murdered."

And Pilate commanded, "Where is the place of the child?"

And the scribe answered, "The parents of the child have taken the child and fled the city."

And Pilate laughed saying, "Fled the city. God destroys my soldiers and the child flees the city. Has God deserted the child for fear of Pilate?"

And the scribe responded saying, "They have fled the city in search of the apostle Simon Peter. They flee not in fear of Pilate they seek Simon Peter for his council. God has not deserted the child. The child is protected by God himself and no man, woman, child, or beast of the earth shall harm the child."

And Pilate commanded, "Where is the place of Simon Peter?"

And the scribe responded, "Simon Peter left the city many months ago. He travels to spread the gospel of the Christ. The place of Simon Peter is not known."

And Pilate commanded of his soldiers and scribes saying, "Caesar must not know of these events. If Caesar knows of these events surely he would send the legions of Rome to find and murder the child. The God of Moses and the Christ protects this child. For the God of Moses destroyed the army of pharaoh and the God of the Christ raised him from the dead. Surely, God would destroy the legions of Rome."

And the soldier spoke saying, "Surely this is not the God of Moses and the Christ for the God of Moses did not destroy pharaoh. The God of Moses sent forth warnings against disobedience. The army of pharaoh was destroyed when they sought to murder the Hebrews. The God of the Christ sent forth John the Baptist that all would know of the coming of the Christ. The God of the Christ did not destroy those that crucified his son. This is not the God of Moses and the Christ."

"No one comes before the child and no prophet has spoken of the child."

"The God of Moses and the Christ was a merciful God. This God shows no mercy to those that seek to harm the child."

And the most elder of the scribes, Titus, stood and spoke saying, "This is the God of Moses and the Christ. God sent Moses to deliver his people from bondage and pharaoh did not heed God's command. God set plagues upon Egypt and pharaoh released his people. It is only when pharaoh sent his army to destroy God's people that God destroyed the army of pharaoh."

"God allowed pharaoh to live that all would know his power."

"God sent the Christ, his only begotten son, to die for the sins of all that all would know the glory of God. For all that follow God and the Christ, although they die, they live. The Christ crucified and raised from the dead that all would know the fulfillment of God's promise."

"The apostles spread the gospel of the Christ and it was God that gave the gift of healing to Simon Peter."

"The child was a leper and a cripple. And the lepers gathered at the gates of Jerusalem to be healed by Simon Peter. Three times the lepers went to the road and three times the crowd drove them back. For the lepers were the unclean of the unclean."

"It was the cry of this child that summoned Simon Peter. And Simon Peter went to the child and held up the child and spoke to the crowd saying, 'All are worthy of God's grace. Not one is unworthy. Not one man, one woman, one child, or one of the unclean of the unclean is unworthy." And the power of God healed the child. And Simon Peter again spoke saying, 'It is the will of God that generations to come will know the power of God through the hands of a child. What was given to me has been given to her." And Simon Peter again spoke saying, 'This child is protected by God himself. No man, woman, child, or beast of the earth shall harm this child. Such is the will of God."

"This child has no power. This child performs no miracles. This child does not heal. This child is not a prophet. God has the power. God performs the miracles. God heals through the hands of the child."

"God has healed many through the hands of the child and God protected the child from beast and man. For those that sought to harm the child were consumed by the fire of God."

"No army can defeat God. No army can harm the child. God himself protects the child. For the fire of God consumes flesh, spear, and sword. Nay, the fire of God consumes even armor for the fire consumes all. There is no ash."

"Only the God of Moses and the Christ could destroy the soldiers of Caesar. Only the God of Moses and the Christ can heal the sick and the infirmed."

"This God is a merciful God. For this God heard the cries of his people in bondage and he delivered them. This God gave his only begotten son to die for all that all may live. And this God gives us the child. For the sick have been healed by his power through the hands of the child. And God has commanded that generations to come will know his power through the hands of a child. And all that are of God and followers of the Christ fear not the child for they seek not to harm the child."

"And God has commanded that no man, woman, child, or beast of the earth shall harm the child. And his fire consumes those that disobey his command."

"And the fire of God that destroyed the man with stone consumed not those with him. For only the man with stone sought to harm the child."

"And the horse of the centurion was not consumed for the horse did not seek to harm the child."

"And the soldiers of drum, horn, and the standard and banner of Caesar were not consumed for they did not seek to harm the child."

"The fire of God consumes all, beast or man, that disobey his command."

"And God has chosen this child. Many have witnessed God heal through the hands of the child. Of this we are certain."

"And the beast harmed the two that went after and they were healed through the hands of the child. Of this we are certain for the beast that killed the one that went before struck down the two that went after. And if God did not heal them through the hands of the child the two that went after would lie dead with the one that went before."

"And the two that went after were charged to guard and protect the child. And the two that went after stood with the child before the guard of Pilate."

"And the two that went after could not defeat the soldiers of Caesar. Of this we are certain."

"And the soldiers of Caesar were defeated. Of this we are certain."

"And only the father of the child witnessed the three serpents consumed by the fire of God. Of this we cannot be certain."

"And only the father of the child and the mother of the child and the two that went after witnessed the beast consumed by the fire of God. Of this we cannot be certain."

"The one that went before lies dead. His body torn as if by a great beast. Of this we can be certain for his body lies near."

רבקה

"And God does not give life through the hands of the child. Of this we can be certain for if God gave life through the hands of the child the one that went before would not lie dead."

"And God does not give death through the hands of the child. Of this we can be certain for all that sought to harm the child, beast or man, were consumed by the fire of God. And the hands of the child touched not beast or man."

"And the fire of God consumed Braka, the seven and twenty, and the man with stone. Of this we are certain. For if it was not so, Braka and the seven and twenty would be amongst us. And the man with stone cannot be found."

"And the fire of God consumed the guard of Pilate. Of this we are certain. For if it was not so, the guard of Pilate would be amongst us."

"And the fire of God consumed the centurion of the guard. Of this we are certain. For if it was not so, the centurion of the guard would be amongst us."

"And the soldiers of drum, horn, and the standard and banner of Caesar were not consumed. Of this we are certain as they are amongst us."

"And the horse of the centurion was not consumed. Of this we are certain for the horse is near and the horse carries no rider."

"No prophet has written of this child and no one comes before. And the child is here. We are but men. We know not the will of God."

"Caesar must not know of these events. For surely Caesar would send the legions of Rome to find and murder the child. And when the soldiers strike at the child, the fire of God will consume them. And Caesar himself would be consumed because it would be he that gave the order to murder the child as the centurion was consumed because he gave the order to murder the child."

"The child has done no harm to Pilate or Caesar. The child has been taken from this city. And those that stand with her seek the counsel of the apostle Simon Peter. The place of Simon Peter is unknown."

"The fate of the child is known only to God."

And Pilate charged his soldiers and scribes saying, "Caesar must not know of these events. For surely he would send the legions of Rome to seek and murder the child and the God of Moses and of the Christ would surely destroy the soldiers of Caesar."

"You will not speak or write of these events. Find all that witnessed these events and destroy them."

And the soldier said, "The crowd that witnessed the consumption of Braka, the seven and twenty, and the man with stone are innocent. And the soldiers of drum, horn, and the standard and banner of Caesar are loyal to Pilate. And the horse of the centurion is but a horse."

And Pilate responded, "Find them all and kill them all. There is to be no one alive, beast or man, who witnessed these events. And do not speak or write of these events. If you speak or write of these events fear not the fire of God. Fear the fire of man. I will have you burned alive in Gehenna."

And Pilate charged them saying, "Leave me now and speak no more and write no more of these events. I will not have the destruction of Rome on my hands."

And all that witnessed these events, beast and man, were gathered together. And they were taken from the city. And all that witnessed these events died by sword and their remains buried in sand.

And the written word of council was torn from its scroll. And the written word was burned. And the ash of the written word was gathered together and buried with the remains of all that witnessed these events.

רבקה

Scroll IX
The Search for the Apostle Simon Peter

And Josep, Mira, the child, and the two who went after traveled to Nazareth seeking the apostle Simon Peter. And not finding the apostle Simon Peter in Nazareth they traveled to Sepphoris.

The writings of Titus

רבקה

Rebecca II
Prologue to Rebecca II

In 1959, an auction of antiquities was held in Milan, Italy. Among the items auctioned was a twelfth century manuscript. The manuscript drew little attention and the auction price was less than five thousand American dollars.

The manuscript is alleged to have been written from several scrolls. The scrolls were alleged to have been written several years after the crucifixion of Jesus Christ. A Roman soldier, who could neither read nor write, dictated this story. The Roman soldier was named Justin.

The actual scrolls could not be produced.

Several experts certified the manuscript to have been written during the twelfth century. However, the manuscript held little value and the story of the scrolls could not be verified.

The manuscript was a curiosity item.

The actual scrolls were alleged to have been written in Aramaic. The manuscript was written in Latin. What follows is an English translation of the manuscript. The manuscript tells the story of Rebecca and the manuscript is titled Rebecca.

רבקה

Rebecca II

Caesar commanded his most fierce soldiers be gathered together unto one legion. And the legion numbered more than three thousand.

And the soldiers were armed in heavy armor. And they carried the gladius and the pilum. And each soldier was to battle. And the legion contained no soldier that did not battle. And the legion contained no horse.

And the legion traveled by ships to the port of Ptolemais. And five of the three thousand and more left the ships. And the five were gone for seven days.

And the five returned to the ships and all were ordered to prepare for battle. And each soldier was prepared for battle. And each soldier that manned the ships was prepared for battle.

And the legion marched to the city of Cana. And the soldiers set their tents near the city after a hill of sand. And the centurions divided the one into three. And the first of the three stood before the second. And the second of the three stood before the third. And each of the three numbered one thousand and more.

And the centurions commanded the soldiers prepare for battle. And the soldiers stood ready for battle.

And the sun rose and the sun set. And the soldiers stood for battle.

And the sun rose and the centurions commanded battle was to begin.

And the soldiers stood ready for battle, one before the other.

And the centurions commanded of them saying, "We battle for Caesar and Rome. We face an enemy greater than any other. The enemy is a God who protects a child. This God defeated the soldiers of Caesar and we avenge their death by murdering the child."

"Caesar commands that we fight to the death. We return in victory for there is no defeat."

And the soldiers readied for battle.

And five crossed a hill of sand. And five stood before the legion of Rome.

And the five were three men, and a woman, and a child. And two of the three men carried sword and shield. And the two with sword and shield drew their swords and held their shields for battle. And the two with sword and shield stood before the woman and child.

And the three thousand and more looked at the five. And they were of concern. For the soldiers of Caesar were killers of men. The soldiers of Caesar were not murderers of women and children.

And the three thousand and more looked at the two men with sword and shield that stood before them.

And the two could not defeat the legion of Rome. And the two stood without fear or concern of death.

And the two that stood before them were of courage.

And the three thousand and more knew not the courage of the two.

And the two that stood before them held allegiance to one greater than Caesar.

And the centurions commanded the soldiers to yell the sound of war. And the soldiers yelled the sound of war. And the centurions commanded the first of the three to charge with spear and shield. And the first of the three charged with spear and shield.

And the centurions charged before the first of the three.

And two stood before the child with sword and shield.

And the centurions neared the child. And the swords of the centurions became as of fire. And the fire consumed them. And the first of the three neared the child and their spears became as of fire. And the fire consumed them.

And the second of the three and the third of the three ceased their yell of war.

And the legion was without command. And two thousand and more stood before the five. And the command to attack was not given.

And one soldier left his stand and went to the five. And the soldier neared the child and placed his spear and sword in sand. And the soldier kneeled before the five and the soldier spoke saying, "I knell not before the child. I knell before the God that protects the child."

"Two stand before the legion of Rome with courage I have not seen in battle. Two stand before the legion of Rome without fear or concern of death."

"I am a soldier of Caesar. I was trained to kill men. I was not trained to murder women or children."

"The God that protects the child is greater than Caesar. The God that protects the child is greater than Rome. I pledge my sword and my life to this God. I pledge my sword and my life to protect the child."

And the soldier stood with the two before the legion of Rome. And he took his spear and sword from sand and he stood ready for battle.

And the soldier stood without fear or concern of death.

And the two thousand and more looked at the six. And no command was given to attack.

And one left his stand. And he ran to the child with sword and shield. And he yelled the sound of war.

And his brethren met him in sand.

And the two soldiers battled in sand. And the first that left his stand struck down his brethren.

And his brethren lay in sand struck down by sword. And the first that left his stand stood ready for battle.

And the two thousand and more looked at the six. And no command was given to attack.

And the first to leave his stand stood to kill his brethren. And his brethren cried out, " Have mercy on your brethren."

And the first to leave his stand raised his sword to kill his brethren.

And the child came between the two.

And the child went to the one that lay in sand and the child placed her hands on the soldier.

And the power of God healed the soldier through the hands of the child. For the soldier that sought to murder the child cried out for mercy. And God heard his cry. And God gave his mercy.

And the soldier that was harmed stood with the first to leave his stand. And the soldier that was harmed knelled. And the soldier spoke saying, " I knell not before the child. I knell before the God that gave his mercy to one that sought to murder the child. I pledge my sword and my life to this God. I pledge my sword and my life to guard and protect the child."

And the two soldiers stood with the two. And four held their swords and shields for battle.

And the two thousand and more witnessed the power of God. For God consumed the first of the three in fire. And the two thousand and more witnessed the grace of God. For God healed the one that sought to murder the child.

For God took the life of the soldier that sought to harm the child. And God gave life to the soldier that asked for mercy.

And the two thousand and more kneeled in sand. And the two thousand and more did not knell to the child. The two thousand and more knelled to the God that protected the child.

And the two thousand and more knelled to the God that gave his grace to the soldier that was harmed.

And the two thousand and more pledged their sword and their life to the God. And the two thousand and more pledged their sword and their life to protect the child.

And the army of Caesar struck their tents. And the legion traveled with the five to the city of Jotapata.

And the army of Caesar traveled before and after the child. And the army before the child numbered one thousand and more. And the army after the child numbered one thousand and more.

And the army that traveled before and after the child was not the army of Caesar. The army that traveled before and after the child was the army of God.

The Soldiers are Baptized unto Christ

And the soldiers traveled with the five to Jotapata. And the father of the child was named Josep. And the mother of the child was named Mira. And the child was named Rebecca.

And the two men who stood before the army of Caesar were brothers. One was named Ahel and the other was named Mahal.

And the five traveled in search of the apostle Simon Peter. And word was spoken of Simon Peter at Jotapata.

And the army of Caesar was the army of God. And the army of God guarded and protected the child. And one thousand and more went before the child. And one thousand and more went after the child.

And they came upon a river. And there were many people at the river. And the people were alarmed when the soldiers appeared. And the people were afraid that the army would murder them.

And one soldier went forth to speak. And the soldier neared the people and he laid his sword and shield to ground. And the soldier spoke saying, "Do not fear us. For among us is a child healed by God and blessed by God. We were sent by Caesar to murder the child and the God that protects the child destroyed my brethren with fire. And the God that destroyed my brethren with fire gave mercy to one that was harmed."

"And we pledged our sword and life to God and we pledged our sword and life to protect the child. And we follow God not for fear of his fire. We follow God for love of the mercy he gave to the one that was harmed."

" We are not the army of Caesar. We are the army of God."

"Those with the child seek the apostle Simon Peter and we march with the child to guard and protect the child."

"Do you know the place of the apostle Simon Peter?"

And one came from the people. And the one that came was the apostle Paul. And the apostle Paul had gathered the people to running water. And the apostle spoke the gospel of Jesus Christ and the apostle baptized the people in running water.

And the apostle Paul spoke saying, "We fear you not. The apostle Simon Peter is not with us. His place is not known. Simon Peter spreads the gospel of the risen Christ as I spread the gospel of the risen Christ."

"Bring forth the child that I may learn of God's blessing to the child. Place your tents among the river's edge and share the food we have."

And the soldier returned to his stand. And the tents were placed near the water's edge. And they shared bread and catches of fish.

And Josep, Mira, and the child were brought to the apostle Paul.

And Josep spoke to the apostle Paul of God healing the child. And Josep spoke of God healing through the hands of the child.

And the child was protected by God himself and God protected the child from three serpents and a beast. And God protected the child from the soldiers of Pilate. And God protected the child from the legion of Caesar.

And the apostle Paul stood among the people and he spoke the gospel of the risen Christ.

And the soldiers gathered to hear his words.

And the apostle Paul spoke of the power of God. And the soldiers wept for they had witnessed the power of God destroy their brethren.

And the apostle Paul spoke of the grace of God. And the soldiers wept for they had witnessed the grace of God. For God gave life to the soldier that was harmed. And the soldier that was harmed sought to murder the child protected by God.

And the apostle Paul spoke of the risen Christ and God's promise to all that believe in Christ and follow Christ.

And the apostle Paul called forth the baptism of Josep, Mira, and Rebecca. And Ahel and Mahal stood to be baptized. And the soldiers stood behind Ahel and Mahal.

And the soldiers stood without concern of rank.

And the apostle Paul baptized Josep, Mira, and Rebecca.

And the apostle Paul baptized Ahel and Mahal.

And the apostle Paul baptized the soldiers. And the soldiers numbered two thousand and more. And the baptism went from sunset to sunrise.

And the apostle Paul spoke to the soldiers saying, "God does not ask for your sword. God does not ask for your life. God does not ask to guard and protect the child. God himself protects the child. And no man, woman, child, or beast of the earth shall harm the child."

"God asks that you cease war on your brethren. God asks that you obey his commands and follow the teachings of his son Jesus Christ. Do these things and though you die, you will live. For at your death, your spirit will leave its flesh and enter the kingdom of God."

And the running water washed away the sin of war. And the running water washed away the sin of man. And the soldiers prayed for God's forgiveness.

And the soldiers removed their armor. And the soldiers gathered their weapons of war. And the armor and weapons of war were taken to the deep of the river.

And the apostle Paul spoke to the soldiers saying, "God has heard your prayers. And God has accepted you unto Christ. Go forth in peace and witness what you have seen and heard."

And the apostle Paul spoke to Josep and Mira saying, "Seek not the council of Simon Peter. God guides Simon Peter and God guides Rebecca. All that you wish to know will be revealed by God in prayer."

And the soldiers took up their tents and they left the river. And Josep, Mira, Rebecca, Ahel, and Mahal left the river.

And the soldier that was harmed by his brethren and healed by God was named Justin. And Justin went with the child.

The Gift is Passed to Another

And the six traveled. And God healed many through the hands of Rebecca. And Rebecca grew in age.

And the child became a young girl. And Rebecca spoke to the five saying; "God has spoken to me in prayer. God sends one to me. And God will heal this one through my hands. And God will heal no other through my hands. For that which was given to me will be given to the one that comes."

"We travel to the city of Tiberias. And near the city is a well of cool water. And we will wait at the well. For the one who God sends will seek the cool water."

And the six traveled to Tiberias. And near the city of Tiberias was a well of cool water. And they waited at the well for the one who God sends.

And there came a man, woman, and an infant child. And the infant child was with fever. And the child cried from the fever. And they stopped at the well to cool the child with water.

And the man spoke to the six saying, "Our son is very ill. We have heard of a child healed by God and blessed by God. We have heard that God heals through the hands of the child."

"Do you have knowledge of the child?"

And Rebecca spoke saying, "I am the one you seek. God has sent your son to me and God has sent me to your son."

And the man and woman kneeled to the ground and the man spoke saying, "We ask the blessing of God that he may heal our son."

And Rebecca spoke saying, "God will heal your son through my hands. And God will heal no other through my hands. For that which was given to me will be taken from me. And that which is taken from me will be given to your son. God will heal through the hands of your son."

And Rebecca held the child and she whispered into the ear of the child. And the child's cries stopped.

And Rebecca spoke saying, "The power of God has healed your son."

And Rebecca passed her hand over the child and she spoke saying, "It is the will of God that generations to come will know the power of God through the hands of a child. What was given to me has been taken from me. And what was taken from me has been given to your son. Your son is protected by God himself. No man, woman, child, or beast of the earth shall harm your son. This is the will of God."

And Rebecca returned the child to his mother.

And Rebecca asked, "What name has been given to your son?"

And the child's mother responded, "His name is Aaron."

And Rebecca spoke saying, "Your son Aaron will serve God. Return to your place and share the blessing which God has given."

And the child was returned to his place. And people came to the place of the child to see the child healed by God and blessed by God. And the sick and the infirmed came to the place of the child. And the sick and the infirmed touched the child and the child touched them. And God healed all who touched the child and were touched by the child.

Aaron Passes the Gift to Another

And God healed through the hands of Aaron. And Aaron grew in age. And Aaron became a young boy.

And when Aaron became a young boy, God sent one to him. And the one sent by God was healed by God through the hands of Aaron. And God healed no other through the hands of Aaron. And God healed through the hands of the one he sent to Aaron.

For that which was given to Rebecca was taken from Rebecca and given to Aaron. And that which was given to Aaron was taken from Aaron and given to another.

For as spoken by the apostle Simon Peter, 'It is the will of God that generations to come will know the power of God through the hands of a child. What was given to me has been given to her. This child is protected by God himself. No man, woman, child, or beast of the earth shall harm this child. This is the will of God."

The Passing of Justin

And Rebecca grew in age. And Rebecca was taken as wife. And no harm came to Rebecca.

And Ahel and Mahal kept guard over Rebecca. For they had been charged to guard and protect her. And Ahel and Mahal kept their faith with God and the child.

For they had charged the beast that sought to harm the child. And the two stood with the child before the soldiers of Caesar.

And Ahel and Mahal grew in age. And Ahel and Mahal died from age.

And Rebecca wept at their death. And the tears of Rebecca were not tears of sorrow. The tears were of joy for their spirit left its flesh and their spirit entered the kingdom of God.

And Josep and Mira grew in age. And Josep and Mira died from age.

And Rebecca wept at their death. And the tears of Rebecca were not tears of sorrow. The tears were of joy for their spirit left its flesh and their spirit entered the kingdom of God.

And Justin grew in age. And Justin died from age.

And Rebecca wept at his death. And the tears of Rebecca were not tears of sorrow. The tears were of joy for his spirit left its flesh and his spirit entered the kingdom of God.

For the soldier that sought to murder the child was harmed by his brethren. And the soldier cried out for mercy. And God heard his cry. And God gave his mercy. And God healed him through the hands of a child.

And God gave death to the soldiers that sought to harm the child. And God gave life to the soldier that cried out for mercy.

And God gave his mercy through the hands of a child.

And that which was given to the child was given to another. And that which was given to another was given to another. And that which was given to another would be given to another.

And the words of Justin were written to scroll. And the scroll of Justin ends with his last spoken words.

"The mercy of God has no end."

The spoken words of Justin

Epilogue to Rebecca II
1945

In 1945, refuges fled before the soldiers of Germany.

Refuges gathered in a large building. The refuges were ill from the cold and lack of food. One refuge was injured from a bomb blast, which injured his leg and arm.

The refuges waited for the allied army to rescue them.

German soldiers found the refuges hiding in the building and the German soldiers believed allied soldiers were among the refuges.

The German soldiers commanded the refuges leave the building. The refuges refused to leave the building. The German soldiers demanded that the refuges leave the building or they would burn the building.

The refuges refused to leave.

What follows is a statement from one of the refuges given to a recorder of the allied army.

"We fled from the German army to the allies. The German soldiers went crazy. They were killing everyone. We hid in a building. There must have been several hundred of us because the building was large and we did not have room to lie down. One man was injured by a bomb and he was bleeding from his leg and arm. He was almost dead."

"I heard that there was a man, woman, and their child with us. And no one knew who they were. One man said the child healed everyone that was sick and the child healed the man injured by the bomb."

"I never saw the child. There were so many of us."

"And I heard the Germans call us out and we all refused because we knew they would kill us."

"And the Germans said if we did not come out they would burn the building. And we were afraid to come out."

"And the Germans said they were going to burn the building and we heard them yell. And we heard the Germans run to the building and we heard the Germans cock their guns to shoot."

"And then we heard silence. And we waited many hours."

"And the doors were broke open. And we screamed because the German soldiers were to kill us. But the doors were broke open by the allies."

"And the German soldiers were gone."

"And outside the building were many trucks that belong to the Germans and one tank that belong to the Germans but there was no Germans."

"And the allies saved us. And the man that was injured by the bomb walked out with us."

רבקה
1980

In 1980, an epidemic of cholera broke out near the city of Tembisa. The people of the area went to the city for medical help.

The people of Tembisa were afraid that the cholera would spread and soldiers were sent to prevent the people from entering the city.

One soldier was placed as a guard to sound an alarm if the people attempted to enter the city.

The people cried for help and there was no one to help them. The soldier on guard was upset by their cries and during the night he left his post.

The following morning, the guard returned to his post and the people had left. The guard was afraid that he would be jailed for leaving his post and the guard searched for the people.

He found a small group walking away from the city. The guard asked them why they left.

What follows is what one of the men in the group told the soldier.

"A man, woman, and a young child came to them in the night. The man told them that God sent the child to them and God will heal them through the child."

"The child touched them and they were healed."

2001 - A Small City in the American Midwest

The elevator sounded the ring for floor 6. The door opened and three people emerged. They walked to the nurse's station and the man introduced himself as Eric. He introduced his wife Irene and their daughter Rachel. He asked to see Samuel.

The nurse stated that Samuel was in room 610. However, Samuel was very ill and he was not expected to survive. Samuel was born premature and his heart did not develop normally. The family was being allowed to be with him, as he was not expected to survive.

The nurse added that only a few visitors were allowed and that they may not be allowed to stay very long.

Eric added, "We won't be long."

The three people walked to room 610. As they approached, the low cry of an infant could be heard. Eric slowly opened the door to see several people in the room. There was a man, woman, a young girl and an infant child in the room. The man was Samuel's father. The woman was Samuel's mother. The young girl was Samuel's older sister.

Samuel's mother held Samuel. The child cried softly.

"Excuse us," Eric stated. "I am Eric. This is my wife Irene and our daughter Rachel. We were told that young Samuel was very ill."

Samuel's mother nodded her head.

Eric continued, "Our daughter was once very ill. God healed our daughter and God blessed our daughter. We are here to share that blessing."

The people in the room seemed perplexed. These people were unknown to them. They were strangers yet their presence brought a peace and a calm.

Samuel's father motioned for them to enter.

Eric and Irene stood near the door. Their daughter Rachel sat on the floor before the mother and the child.

The child continued to cry. Samuel's mother spoke saying, " Our baby was born premature and his heart did not develop normally. He has many problems. The doctors have operated but there is little hope he will recover. The doctors believe he doesn't have much time to live."

"We have prayed to God for a miracle."

Rachel spoke saying, "God has heard your prayers and God has sent me to your son. God will heal your son through my hands and God will heal no other through my hands. For that which was given to me will be taken from me. And that which is taken from me will be given to your son. God will heal through the hands of your son."

The family looked at Rachel.

Rachel held out her arms and she spoke to the mother saying, "May I hold your son?"

Samuel's mother was reluctant to hand her son to the young girl. Her husband spoke softly, "Let her hold him."

Samuel's mother carefully placed Samuel in Rachel's arms. Samuel cried softly.

Rachel held the baby close and she whispered into his ear. The cries stopped.

Rachel looked at the child's mother and the child's father and she said, "The power of God has healed your son."

Rachel passed her hand over Samuel's head and body. She looked upward and whispered. She then looked at the mother and the father and said, "It is the will of God that generations to come will know the power of God through the hands of a child. What was given to me has been taken from me. What was taken from me has been given to your son."

Rachel again looked upward and she spoke saying, "Your son is protected by God himself. No man, woman, child, or beast of the earth shall harm your son. This is the will of God."

Rachel handed Samuel to his mother.

Rachel again spoke saying; "Your son Samuel will serve God. Return to your place and share the blessing which God has given."

רבקה
The Ten Scrolls

The Command of Pilate

And Pilate responded, "Find them all and kill them all. There is to be no one alive, beast or man, who witnessed these events. And do not speak or write of these events. If you speak or write of these events fear not the fire of God. Fear the fire of man. I will have you burned alive in Gehenna."

And Pilate charged them saying, "Leave me now and speak no more and write no more of these events. I will not have the destruction of Rome on my hands."

And all who witnessed these events, beast and man, were gathered together. And they were taken from the city. And all who witnessed these events died by sword and their remains buried in sand.

And the written word of council was torn from its scroll. And the written word was burned. And the ash of the written word was gathered together and buried with the remains of all who witnessed these events.

The Soldiers Come to Titus

And many days passed.

And Titus walked in the garden of Pilate and five soldiers came to him.

And one of the five soldiers spoke saying, "We heard your words before Pilate. Such words we have not heard before. Do you have knowledge of this God of whom you spoke?"

Titus replied, "Yes. I have read many scrolls. I know of men who speak of God."

And the soldier asked, "Will you teach us of this God?"

Titus replied, "Why do you wish to know of God?"

The soldier replied, "This God performs miracles of which no man can perform. We know not of the miracles of Moses and the Christ. We know of the miracles of the child."

Titus replied, "Pilate has commanded no man speak or write of those events. If Pilate has knowledge of such words, you will be burned alive in Gehenna."

The solder replied, "We heard Pilate's command and we obey Pilate's command. Pilate gave no command of this God."

And Titus replied, "I will teach you of God. You will come to my place when the sun sets."

And the five soldiers waited for the sun to set. And when the sky was dark, they went to the place of Titus.

And the place of Titus is filled with many scrolls for Titus is a scribe. And Titus knows of many languages and Titus writes in these many languages. And Titus read to them from many scrolls.

And the soldiers left the place of Titus before the sun rose.

And each day, the sun set.

And each night, the soldiers went to the place of Titus.

And each night, Titus read to them from many scrolls. And the soldiers learned of God.

And each morning, the soldiers left the place of Titus before the sun rose.

And one night, the five soldiers came to the place of Titus. And one soldier spoke saying, "All men should know of these things. We cannot read or write. If you will write these things we will take them to men who can read."

And Titus spoke saying, "What do you want me to write?"

And the soldier replied, "The child."

And Titus replied, "Pilate commands no man write of those events."

And the soldier replied, "We have spoken among ourselves. We know of Pilate's command. We know of what will happen to us if Pilate learns of our plan."

And Titus asked, "You know of Pilate's command and you will risk your life?"

And the soldier replied, "Of these events, men should know."

And Titus went to a cabinet made of wood. And Titus opened the cabinet. And within the cabinet lay a skin.

And Titus took the skin from the cabinet and he laid the skin before the five soldiers. And Titus opened the skin and within the skin was a scroll.

And Titus spoke saying, "This scroll was written many years ago. It was given to me and entrusted to my care. I have hidden this scroll from those who could read its words."

"Within this scroll is the story of the child. Within this scroll is the story of events to come."

The soldier spoke saying, "And you spoke not of the child?"

Titus replied, "I did not believe the words of the scroll."

And Titus spoke saying, "Come to my place in three days."

The Plan of Titus

And the five soldiers waited three days. And on the third day, they went to the place of Titus.

And Titus lay before them ten scrolls.

And Titus spoke saying, "I have written of the events of which Pilate has commanded no man write."

"Nine scrolls tell of these events. The tenth scroll is the one to which I have held for many years."

"The tenth scroll foretells the child and this scroll tells of events to come."

"You will each take two scrolls. You will journey to the city of Qumran. You will ask to speak to a scribe named Julian. You will tell Julian these scrolls come from me."

"Julian will copy these scrolls. There will be six each of the ten. Julian will keep one of each of the ten. You will each be given one of the ten. Julian will send each of you to another."

And the scrolls were divided into two. And each soldier was given two. And the soldiers left the place of Titus.

And the soldiers of Pilate waited outside the place of Titus.

And the soldiers brought Titus and the five soldiers before Pilate. And the ten scrolls were placed before Pilate.

And Pilate read the nine scrolls.

And Pilate read the tenth scroll.

And Pilate's face looked white as he read the tenth scroll.

And Pilate commanded of Titus saying, "These men cannot read or write. Only you could have written these scrolls."

And Titus spoke saying, "I wrote nine of the ten."

And Pilate commanded, "Where did you get the tenth scroll?"

And Titus replied, "It was written many years ago. It was entrusted to my care. I have held it for many years."

And Pilate held up the tenth scroll before Titus.

And Pilate commanded saying, "You held great knowledge. You did not speak?"

And Titus spoke saying, "I did not believe."

And Pilate commanded saying. "Do you believe now?"

And Titus spoke saying, "Yes."

And Pilate commanded saying, "Do you know what you write?"

And Titus spoke saying, "I write of things man should know."

And Pilate spoke saying, "You write of things man should not know. For if man knows of these things, man would rebel against Caesar and Rome."

And Pilate spoke saying, "You know of my command. These ten scrolls share your fate."

And Pilate commanded an earthen jar be brought forth. And a large jar was brought before Pilate. And Pilate commanded the ten scrolls placed in the jar and sealed. And the ten scrolls were placed in the jar and the jar was sealed with slip.

And Pilate commanded, "Take these men and this jar to Gehenna. Take them to where the fire burns greatest. Bind their legs and their arms. Bind their mouths. Throw them into the fire and throw the jar into the fire with them."

Pilate Burns the Tenth Scroll

And the soldiers took the six men and the jar. And the soldiers were to leave Pilate.

And Pilate commanded, "Stop!"

And the soldiers stopped.

And Pilate commanded, "Bring the tenth scroll to me."

And the jar was unsealed. And the tenth scroll was handed to Pilate.

And Pilate commanded a great iron brazier be brought before him. And a great iron brazier was brought before Pilate.

And Pilate commanded wood burned in the brazier.

And the soldiers placed large blocks of wood in the brazier. And the fire blazed hot.

And Pilate read the tenth scroll. And Pilate commanded, "More wood."

And more wood was placed in the brazier. And the fire of the brazier was hot and the smoke was great in the room.

And Pilate read the tenth scroll. And Pilate commanded, "More wood."

And more wood was placed in the brazier. And the fire leapt high in the room.

And Pilate commanded, "I will see for myself the destruction of the tenth scroll."

And Pilate handed the scroll to a soldier. And the soldier threw the scroll into the brazier. And the scroll burned quickly from the heat and the fire.

And Pilate commanded, "More wood."

And more wood was placed in the brazier. And the fire leapt high in the room.

And Pilate commanded the jar be sealed. And the jar was sealed with slip.

And the soldiers took Titus, the five soldiers, and the jar to the valley of Gehenna. And the soldiers searched for the fire, which burned greatest. And the six were bound. And the six were thrown into the fire. And the earthen jar was thrown into the fire.

And the fire in the brazier burned. And when the fires began to cool, more wood was placed in the brazier.

And the fire burned for seven days and seven nights. And the ash of the tenth scroll was mixed with the ash of the wood, which burned.

And the fires cooled after the seventh day. And the ashes from the wood and the scroll were gathered together. And the ashes from the wood and the scroll were spread upon the ground.

The Deliverance of Evan
Prologue - The Deliverance of Evan

Several years after the resurrection of our Lord and Savior Jesus Christ, the tax collectors of Caesar brought much suffering to the people of Hebron. The soldiers of the tax collectors were cruel to the people and many were imprisoned unjustly.

There came from the people two men who protected the weak from the tax collectors. These men fought to protect those unable to protect themselves. These two men were Evan and his son Jacob.

Evan and Jacob lead a small group of eleven men. These men fought to protect the families and the homes of the people. These men helped those harmed by the tax collector.

Evan and Jacob were fierce in battle. Jacob commanded the sword and no man was his equal. The soldiers of the tax collector feared battle with Jacob for no man had defeated Jacob.

Jacob was born a cripple. His leg was twisted.

The soldiers of the tax collector took Evan prisoner. Evan was to be taken before Pontius Pilate that he might be judged. The sentence would be death.

This story tells of the young boy Jacob and how the power of God healed Jacob. This story also tells of the angel of God who delivered the father of Jacob, Evan.

This story also concerns the child Rebecca. Rebecca was a leper and a cripple. The power of God healed Rebecca through the hands of the apostle Simon Peter. And Simon Peter spoke saying, ' It is the will of God that generations to come will know the power of God through the hands of a child. What was given to me has been given to her. This child is protected by God himself. No man, woman, child, or beast of the earth shall harm this child. This is the will of God."

And God blessed Rebecca. And God healed through the hands of the child.

In this story, Rebecca was taken to Hebron to the place of Cephus. Cephus was of God and a follower of the Christ. Cephus fell ill. And Cephus was too ill to travel to the child. The child was taken to Cephus.

The story is titled - The Deliverance of Evan.

Jacob Battles to Free Rebecca

And the child was taken to the place of Cephus, as Cephus was too ill to travel. And the power of God healed Cephus through the hands of the child.

And the child stayed many days at the place of Cephus. And many came to the place of Cephus to see the child healed by God and blessed by God. And the ill and the infirmed came to the place of Cephus. And the ill and the infirmed touched the child and the child touched them. And God healed all who touched the child and were touched by the child.

And Josep, Mira, and Rebecca were to leave the place of Cephus. And there was a beast that roamed the hill. And the beast had killed cattle and man. And Cephus charged three men to guard and protect the child. And the three men were brothers. And the three men were Jaykal, Ahel, and Mahal. And Jaykal was the eldest. And Mahal was the youngest. And the three men carried spear, sword, and shield.

And Jaykal walked before the child and Ahel and Mahal walked after the child.

And they went to the road that leads to the place of the child. And a young boy stood in the road. And the young boy was twelve years in age. And the young boy was a cripple. And the young boy held a crutch made from the branch of the olive tree.

And the young boy barred their path.

And the young boy commanded of them, "Release the child!"

And Ahel and Mahal came forward. And Ahel and Mahal stood with Jaykal.

And the young boy commanded of them, "Release the child!"

And the young boy stood before the three brothers. And the three brothers were armed with spear, sword, and shield. And the young boy held no weapon save the crutch made from the olive tree. And the young boy was great with courage.

And the young boy took the crutch from under his arm and he held the crutch in air. And the young boy commanded of them, "Release the child!"

And the three brothers knew not of the command. And the three brothers stood before the young boy.

And the young boy yelled to Josep and Mira saying, "Take the child to safety! I will battle these men!"

And the young boy yelled the sound of battle. And the young boy charged the three brothers with his crutch.

And the young boy struck the shield of Jaykal with his crutch. And he yelled to Josep and Mira saying, "Run to town! There are many who will protect you."

And the young boy struck the shield of Ahel and Mahal with his crutch. And the young boy battled with his crutch of olive wood.

And Jaykal, Ahel, and Mahal did not return the blows. And the three brothers held their shields before them. And the young boy struck great blows against their shields. And the young boy drove them back with his blows.

And the young boy yelled to Josep and Mira, "Take the child and run!"

And the young boy struck the shield of Ahel with his crutch made from the branch of the olive tree. And the blow tore the shield from the arm of Ahel.

And the three brothers released their spears. And Jaykal took the crutch from the young boy. And the young boy beat the shield of Jaykal with his bear hands. And the young boy yelled to Josep and Mira saying, "Take the child and run!"

And the young boy struck great blows against the shield of Jaykal. And the young boy drove Jaykal back.

And Jaykal and Mahal released their shields and the three brothers took hold of the young boy. And the young boy yelled to Josep and Mira, "Take the child to safety!"

And the three brothers held the young boy and Josep came to the young boy. And Josep spoke saying, "Why do you battle these men?"

And the young boy yelled, "These men seek to harm the child. They arrest the child."

And Josep spoke saying, "We are not at arrest. These men were charged by Cephus to guard and protect us."

And the young boy yelled, "These men carry weapons of war."

And Josep spoke saying, "These men carry weapons of war to protect us from the beast that roams the hill."

And the young boy yelled, "These men arrest you. Run to the town! There are many who will protect you."

And Mira came forth and spoke saying, "Josep speaks the truth. These men guard and protect us. We are not at arrest."

And the young boy stopped his struggle. And the three brothers released the young boy. And Mahal handed the crutch made from the olive tree to the young boy.

And Ahel spoke saying, "I know of this boy. This boy came to the place of Cephus. The young boy witnessed God heal others."

And Josep spoke saying, "Is this true? Did you come to the place of Cephus to be healed by God?"

And the young boy spoke saying, "It is true. I came to the place of Cephus to witness for myself if God healed through the hands of the child. I witnessed God heal others through the hands of the child."

"I did not come to the place of Cephus to be healed by God. I came to ask that the child be brought to my mother."

And Josep spoke saying, "What is your name?"

And the young boy spoke saying, "My name is Jacob."

And Mira spoke saying, "Jacob, why did you battle these men?"

And Jacob spoke saying, "My mother is very ill. I heard of a child healed by God and blessed by God. God heals through the hands of the child. And word came that the child was at the place of Cephus. And many went to the place of Cephus to ask for God's blessing. And I went to the place of Cephus to witness for myself if this was true."

"And I witnessed many people healed by God through the hands of the child. And I returned to my place to bring my mother that she may be healed. And my mother is too ill to walk. And I tried to carry her to the place of Cephus. And I am not of strength to carry her."

"And I came to the place of Cephus to ask that the child be brought to my place. And I witnessed these three men armed with spear, sword, and shield. And these three men surrounded the child. And one went before the child and two went after. And I believed the child at arrest."

"And I feared these men would murder the child."

רבקה

"And I ran for help. And there was no man near to help. And I ran to the road that I might bar their path. And I battled these men to save the child."

And Jaykal spoke saying, "How did you hope to defeat us with your crutch of olive wood?"

And Jacob spoke saying, "My only weapon was my crutch. I would battle with my bear hands to save the child."

And Josep spoke saying, "You battled these men with a crutch of wood and your leg is twisted. How did you hope to defeat these men in battle?"

And Jacob spoke saying, "I asked God for strength to battle these three men. I asked God to give me strength that I might free the child. I battled to save the child. My leg is of no concern."

And Ahel spoke saying, "I have not witnessed such skill in battle. No man has torn the shield from my arm."

And Mahal spoke saying, "No man has struck such blows."

And Jaykal spoke saying, "My brothers speak truth. I have not witnessed such skill in battle. No man has struck such blows."

"You believed the child was at arrest and you risked your life to save the child. You are a great warrior. If you battled with sword, truly you would defeat us."

And Mira spoke saying, "Where is your father?"

And Jacob spoke saying, "My father is at arrest. He was taken many days ago. My father could not pay the tax and he was taken. I do not know the place of my father."

And Mira spoke saying, "Where is your mother?"

And Jacob spoke saying, "My mother is at my place. She is very ill. I came to ask that the child be brought to my mother. If it is the will of God, God will heal my mother through the hands of the child."

And Josep spoke saying, "You are great with courage for you sought to save the child. You battled three men with a crutch of wood. And the three men were armed with spear, sword, and shield. And the crutch of wood was taken from you. And you battled with your hands."

"And you are young in age. And you battled with a twisted leg."

"Come to the child and touch the child. If it is the will of God, the child will touch you. The power of God will heal your leg."

And Jacob spoke saying, "My leg is of no concern. I ask that the child be taken to my mother."

And Mira spoke saying, "Take us to your place."

And they went to the place of Jacob. And the place was far. And they came to the home of Jacob. And the sun was near its setting. And they entered the home and the mother of Jacob lay near death.

Elizabeth Healed by God

And the mother of Jacob was named Elizabeth. And Elizabeth lay in bed with fever. And she was near death. And Rebecca was brought near Elizabeth that Elizabeth may touch the child.

And Elizabeth could not touch the child as she was near death. And Rebecca went to the bed of Elizabeth and Rebecca held the hand of Elizabeth. And the power of God healed Elizabeth through the hands of Rebecca.

And Elizabeth came from her bed.

And Josep spoke to Jacob saying, "God has blessed your home. Come, touch Rebecca that God will heal your leg."

And Jacob spoke saying, "God has blessed our home for God has healed my mother through the hands of Rebecca. The child is safe. I ask nothing for myself. The tax collector took my father from us. I ask God to return my father to us."

And Josep spoke saying, "Of this I have no knowledge."

And Jacob went to the door and he opened the door. And the sun was setting. And Jacob again spoke saying, "Of my leg I have no concern."

And they watched the sun set. And being late in the day they slept.

And the sun rose. And Elizabeth prepared food of bread. And they ate the bread. And it was time to leave for they were to return to the place of the child.

And Josep spoke to Jacob saying, "God has blessed your home. Come, touch the child and the child will touch you. God will heal your leg through the hands of Rebecca."

And Jacob spoke saying, "I ask nothing for myself, I ask God that my father be returned to us."

And Rebecca went to the door and she opened the door. And a shout was heard. And Evan, the father of Jacob, was running toward the door.

And Evan came into the home. And he held Elizabeth and Jacob. And Evan spoke that God sent his angel to deliver him. And Evan spoke of his release.

The Angel of God Delivers Evan

"There were ten and two of us. And we were bound with rope that we could not flee. We were to be taken to Pilate that we would be judged. And we feared the sentence would be death."

"And the sun was setting. And the fires of the camp were lit. And the guards brought bread for food."

"And soldiers came to us. And a soldier spoke of a soldier who rode into camp. And the soldier who rode into camp commanded that the officer be brought before him. And the officer came to him. And the soldier commanded that the prisoners be assembled before him. And the officer ordered that the prisoners be brought forth."

"And the soldiers took us before the soldier who rode into camp."

"And the soldier was unlike any I have seen. And the soldier was large. And the color of his horse was white like the cloud."

"And the soldier wore a breast plate of gold and silver. And upon his head was a helmet of gold and silver. And his hair was of dark black and his beard was of dark black. And his eyes were as fire."

"And his saddle shone like the sun. And the bridle of his horse was of leather I have not seen."

"And the hilt of his sword was of gold. And the soldier carried no shield."

"And we were assembled before the soldier. And the soldier dismounted his horse."

"And we lowered our heads before the soldier. And the soldier walked among us. And the soldier stopped before me."

"And the soldier spoke saying, 'What is your name?"

"And I answered, 'My name is Evan."

"And the soldier spoke saying,' your son Jacob is great with courage."

"Of your son, God is pleased."

"And the soldier spoke saying, 'I have been sent by God to deliver you."

"And the soldier returned to his horse and the soldier mounted his horse."

"And the soldier commanded of the officer saying, 'Has any man taken sword against Caesar or Rome?"

"The officer answered, 'No man has taken sword against Caesar or Rome."

"The soldier commanded, 'Why are these men held captive?"

"The officer answered, 'These men spoke against the tax collector."

"The soldier commanded, 'What words were spoken?"

"The officer answered, 'These men spoke that they could not pay the tax for to pay the tax would leave their families hungry for food. These men did not pay the tax."

"The soldier commanded, 'Where do you take these men?"

"The officer answered, 'These men are to be taken before Pilate that Pilate may judge them."

"The soldier commanded, 'Pilate need not judge these men. God judged these men. These men did not seek to raise sword against Caesar or Rome. These men sought to protect their families and their homes."

"Of these men, God is pleased."

"Bring food and water to each man that he may not hunger or thirst on his journey home."

"And the soldier commanded, 'Free these men!"

"The officer asked, 'Who orders their release?"

"And the soldier drew his sword from its sheath. And the sword was of silver and gold. And the sword burned with white fire. And the fire covered the soldier. And the fire covered his horse. And the sword, soldier, and horse burned in white fire."

"And the soldier held the sword of white fire in air and the soldier commanded saying, 'No man orders their release!"

"God commands these men set free!"

"And we trembled and fell to our knees. For before us was not a soldier of Caesar. Before us was the angel of God."

"And many soldiers released their weapons and ran from the camp. And the officer ordered that our ropes be untied to set us free. And the officer ordered rations of food and water to be given to each man. And the soldiers hurried to untie our ropes and those ropes that could not be untied were cut by the knife of the soldier."

"And each man was untied. And each man ran from the camp, as he was untied. And I ran from the camp when my ropes were untied. And the ten and two of us were set free. And we ran from the camp."

"And the angel of God moved his horse before the soldiers. And the angel of God held his sword of white fire in air that no soldier would follow."

"And no soldier could defeat the angel of God. And no army could defeat the angel of God. For the angel of God and his horse burned with the fire of God. And the fire of God did not consume the angel and his horse. For the angel of God commanded the fire of God."

"And no soldier raised his sword in battle. And no soldier followed. And no soldier was harmed. For the soldiers obeyed the command of God."

"And the soldiers ran from the camp. And the camp was barren."

"And I witnessed the angel of God return his sword to its sheath. And the white fire left the angel of God and his horse. And I witnessed the angel of God ride his horse from the camp."

"And I ran to my home thanking God for his blessing. And I neared our home and the door opened. And when I saw the child, I knew the child was of God."

רבקה
God Heals Jacob

And Evan, Elizabeth, and Jacob went with the child to where the road leads to the place of the child.

And Joseph spoke to Jacob saying, "God has blessed you. For the power of God healed your mother and the angel of God delivered your father. Come to the child and touch the child that your leg will be healed."

And Jacob spoke saying, "God has blessed our home two times. Of my leg I have no concern."

And Mira spoke saying, "Jacob, God has found favor with you. Come, touch the child and the child will touch you. God will heal your leg through the hands of Rebecca."

And Jacob spoke saying, "I ask no more of God. The child is safe and God has blessed me two times."

"If it is the will of God that my leg will be healed, my crutch will be taken from me and cast away."

And Rebecca went to Jacob. And Rebecca held the crutch with one hand and she touched the leg of Jacob with the other hand. And the power of God healed the leg of Jacob through the hand of Rebecca.

And Rebecca pulled the crutch from Jacob. And Rebecca released the crutch to the ground.

The Journey Home

And the six walked on the road to the place of the child. And the three brothers were charged by Cephus to guard and protect the child. And Jaykal went before the child. And Ahel and Mahal went after the child.

רבקה

רבקה

The Plot of Satan

God Heals Rebecca

And word came that a great healer was in Jerusalem. And the great healer healed all who were sick and infirmed. And the great healer made blind men to see and cripples to walk. And the great healer was to leave the city.

And many traveled to Jerusalem to see the great healer and to be healed by him. And the lepers came to the city. And the lepers were driven from the city for the lepers were the unclean of the unclean.

And the lepers waited at the gates of the city for the great healer to pass. And as they waited their numbers increased.

And the great healer came to the gates of the city. And the road was filled of the sick and the infirmed. And as the great healer passed, all within his reach were healed. And those not near to touch the great healer reached for his shadow. And those who touched the shadow of the great healer were healed.

And the lepers went to the road and the crowd drove them back. For the lepers were the unclean of the unclean. Three times the lepers went to the road and three times they were driven back.

And the crowd cheered for they were healed. And the lepers wept for they were not healed.

And the great healer passed on the road and he heard the cry of a young child. And the great healer stopped and commanded all to be silent. And all were silent. And the only sound was the cry of a young child.

And the great healer left the road and went to where the child lay. And the great healer stood before the child. And the child was a leper and a cripple. And the great healer stood among the lepers.

And the great healer took the child and held up the child for all to see and he spoke to the crowd saying, "All are worthy of God's grace. Not one man, one woman, one child, or one of the unclean of the unclean is unworthy."

And the great healer whispered in the ear of the child and the child's cries stopped.

רבקה

And again the great healer held up the child for all to see and again he spoke to the crowd saying, "The power of God has healed this child."

And the great healer passed his hand over the child and a third time he held up the child for all to see. And a third time he spoke to the crowd saying, "It is the will of God that for generations to come all with know the power of God through the hands of a child. What was given to me has been given to her. This child is protected by God himself. No man, woman child, or beast of the earth shall harm this child. This is the will of God."

And the great healer gave the child to the parents and he touched them and he blessed them. And he spoke to them saying, "Your child will serve God. Return to your place and share the blessing which God has given."

And the great healer did not return to the road. The great healer walked among the lepers. And as he walked among them he touched them. He touched them all. And as he touched them they were healed. All were healed

And the great healer returned to the road. And the crowd cheered for all had been healed.

And the child was returned to her place. And people came to the place of the child to see the child healed by God and blessed by God.

And the sick and the infirmed came to the place of the child. And they touched the child and the child touched them. And God healed all who touched the child and were touched by the child.

And Satan witnessed these events. And Satan was angered. And Satan plotted to destroy the child.

The Plot of the Three Serpents

And Satan summoned three to him. And three came to him. And before the three sat a vessel. And Satan commanded of the three, "Drink from this vessel!"

And the three drank from the vessel.

And Satan commanded saying, "Within the vessel is the venom of many serpents. No man can survive the strike of this venom."

"I send you to a place of stone. You will wait among the stone for a child. I will lure the child to you."

"When the child comes near, you will strike the child."

And the three became serpents.

And Satan placed the three serpents in a place of stone. And the three serpents lay among the stone. And the three serpents waited for the child to come near.

Satan Lures the Child to Stone

And the child played before her place.

And there came a butterfly. And the butterfly was bright with many colors. And the wings of the butterfly were colors of yellow, red, gold, green, and blue. And the butterfly flew near the child. And the butterfly flew upwards and downwards. And the child laughed at the butterfly.

And the butterfly lighted near the child. And the child came to the butterfly. And when the child neared the butterfly, the butterfly flew into the air.

And the butterfly flew near the child. And the butterfly flew upwards and downwards. And the child laughed at the butterfly.

And the butterfly lighted near the child. And the child came to the butterfly. And when the child neared the butterfly, the butterfly flew into the air.

And the butterfly lighted near the child. And the child came to the butterfly. And when the child neared the butterfly, the butterfly flew into the air.

And the child enjoyed the game of the butterfly. And the child laughed at the butterfly. And the child followed the butterfly.

And the child followed the butterfly far from her place. And when the child was far from her place, the butterfly flew high into the air. And the butterfly flew away.

And the child was far from her place. And the child knew not her place. And the child wandered searching for her place.

Three Serpents Consumed by the Fire of God

And the child wandered from her place to a place of stone.

And among the stone three serpents lay.

And when the child neared the stone the three serpents came to the child. And the three serpents went before and after the child.

And Josep missing the child called to the child. And hearing not the child, Josep searched for the child.

And Josep found the child near stone. And three serpents went before and after the child.

And Josep called for the child. And the child came to Josep. And the three serpents barred the path.

And the three serpents moved around the child. And the three serpents whipped their tails at the child. And the three serpents barred their fangs to the child.

And the child being young of age knew not the danger of the three serpents. And the child cried not.

And the three serpents neared the child. And the first of the three struck at the child. And the first of the three became as of fire. And the fire consumed the serpent.

And the second and third of the three struck at the child. And the second and third of the three became as of fire. And the fire consumed the serpents.

And Josep held the child and spoke to the child saying, "God himself protected you. For the three serpents were consumed in fire. And only the fire of God could consume the three serpents before they struck."

And Satan witnessed this event. And Satan was angered. And Satan plotted to destroy the child.

The Plot of the Beast

And Satan summoned one to him. And one came to him. And before the one lay a skin of fur. And Satan commanded of him, "Take this skin and cover yourself!"

And the one took the skin and covered himself.

And Satan commanded saying, "No weapon of man will pierce this skin. No spear, sword, arrow, or stone from a sling will harm you."

"I send you to Hebron and near Hebron are great hills. I will give you command of these hills."

"You will wait for a child. The child will come to you. When the child comes near, you will strike down the child and all who stand with her."

And the one became a great beast.

And Satan placed the beast in the hills of Hebron. And the beast roamed the hills of Hebron. And the beast killed cattle and man. And the beast waited for the child to come.

The Beast Consumed by the Fire of God

And Josep, Mira, and the child traveled to Hebron to the place of Cephus. For Cephus was of God and a follower of the Christ.

And Cephus lay on cloth. And the body of Cephus bears the marks of sores. And Cephus was near death.

And Cephus asked of Josep and Mira that the child may come near. And Cephus held out his hand to the child and he touched the child. And the child touched the hand of Cephus.

And God healed Cephus through the hands of the child as he was of God and a follower of the Christ. And the family and the child stayed at the place of Cephus for many days.

And the family and the child were to return to their place.

And Cephus stopped them and spoke to them saying, "A beast roams the hill and this beast has killed cattle and man. Take these three men and they will protect your journey home."

And the three men were armed with spear, sword, and shield. And Cephus charged them to guard and protect Josep, Mira, and the child. And one went before and two went after.

And they approached a place of wood and stone and the beast charged the one who went before and struck him down. And the two who went after charged the beast with spear and sword. And they struck the beast with spear and sword and the beast was not harmed. And the beast struck down the two who went after.

And Josep, Mira, and the child stood before the beast.

And the child being young of age knew not the danger of the beast. And the child cried not.

And the beast roared. And the beast pawed the ground. And the beast bared its teeth.

And the beast charged the child. And the beast neared the child. And the beast became as of fire. And the fire consumed the beast.

And Satan witnessed this event. And Satan was angered. And Satan plotted to destroy the child.

Satan Summoned before God

God summoned Satan before him.

And Satan left his place and came before God.

God commanded, "It is my will generations to come will know my power through the hands of a child. I healed this child. I blessed this child. I protect this child. No man, woman, child, or beast of the earth shall harm this child."

"Two times you sought to harm this child. Two times I protected this child."

"This child is the first. There is no last."

"I command you seek not to harm this child or any child whom I protect!"

"I command you seek not to harm any who stand with this child or any child whom I protect! Those who stand with the child follow my will."

And Satan lowered his head before God. And Satan spoke saying, "I obey your commands."

The Command of Satan

And Satan returned to his place. And Satan commanded all whom he commands to assemble before him.

And all whom Satan commands assembled before him.

And Satan spoke saying, "It is the will of God generations to come will know his power through the hands of a child. God has chosen a child and God protects this child. God commands no man, woman, child, or beast of the earth shall harm this child."

"Two times I sought to destroy this child. Two times God protected this child."

"This child is the first. There is no last."

"God commands I seek not to harm this child or any child whom he protects. God commands I seek not to harm those who stand with this child or any child whom he protects."

And Satan commanded of those whom he commands, "You will obey God's commands as I obey God's commands!"

And Satan spoke saying, "Man knows good and evil. Those men who know good will not seek to harm the child. There are many men who know evil. And among those men who know evil, there will be men who will seek to harm the child."

"The evil in these men will not come from me. The evil in these men will come from within themselves."

And Satan dismissed all whom he commands.

The Spirit of Jaykal Brought Unto the Kingdom of God

And the three men who were charged by Cephus to guard and protect the child were brothers. And the three brothers were Jaykal, Ahel, and Mahal. And Jaykal was the eldest. And Mahal was the youngest.

And Jaykal walked before the child and Ahel and Mahal walked after the child. And the beast struck down Jaykal, Ahel, and Mahal.

And Ahel and Mahal were harmed by the beast. And Jaykal lay dead from the beast. And the body of Jaykal was torn by the beast.

And God healed Ahel and Mahal through the hands of the child.

And God commanded the spirit of Jaykal leave its flesh. And the spirit of Jaykal left its flesh.

And the angels of God surrounded the spirit of Jaykal.

And the angels of God brought the spirit of Jaykal unto the kingdom of God.

רבקה

Jerron

Jerron

And Jerron was wealthy and Jerron commanded many servants. And Jerron fell ill.

And word of the child healed by God and blessed by God came to the ear of Jerron. And word was spoken of the child at the place of Cephus.

And Jerron commanded his servants to take him to the place of Cephus. And the servants lifted his bed and carried him to the place of Cephus.

And the doors of the home of Cephus are closed. And many waited before the door. For the door would be opened that all may enter and ask God's blessing.

And Jerron was the last. And Jerron commanded his servants take him to the door. And the servants brought Jerron to the door and Jerron was the first.

And the doors were opened. And Cephus commanded of all, "Come into my home. Seek the blessing of God."

And Jerron was the first. And the servants of Jerron brought Jerron before the child.

And Jerron touched the child. And the child did not touch Jerron. And Jerron was not healed for God knew the heart of Jerron. And Jerron was not of God and a follower of the Christ. For Jerron cared not for those of misfortune.

And Jerron commanded his servants return him to his place. And the servants returned Jerron to his place.

The Gift of Food and Cloth

And Jerron called forth his servants. And Jerron commanded food and cloth be gathered together. And the servants gathered food and cloth.

And Jerron commanded of the servants, "Take this food and cloth to the place of Cephus. Present these gifts before the child.

רבקה

When God sees my great gift, the child will touch me and I will be healed."

And the servants brought food and cloth to the place of Cephus. And the servants lay the gifts before the child. And Josep spoke saying, "God does not ask for food and cloth."

And Josep handed the gifts to several men. And Josep asked the gifts be given to those of misfortune. And the men went outside the place of Cephus. And the men handed food and cloth to those who waited.

And one of the men was named Ahel. And Ahel worked for Cephus. And Ahel gave food to those who waited. And there was a young boy among those who waited. And the young boy was a cripple. And the young boy carried a crutch made from the branch of the olive tree.

And Ahel handed food to the young boy. And the young spoke saying, "My needs are small. There is one whose needs are greater. Give my food to another."

And Ahel gave the food to another. And the food and cloth were given to those of misfortune.

And the servants of Jerron witnessed the food and cloth given to others. And the servants returned to Jerron. And when the servants returned to Jerron, the day was ended.

And the sun rose.

And Jerron commanded his servants take him to the place of Cephus. And the servants lifted his bed and carried him to the place of Cephus.

And the doors of the home of Cephus are closed. And many waited before the door. For the door would be opened that all may enter and ask God's blessing.

And Jerron was the last. And Jerron commanded his servants take him to the door. And the servants brought Jerron to the door and Jerron was the first.

And the doors were opened. And Cephus commanded of all, "Come into my home. Seek the blessing of God."

And Jerron was the first. And the servants of Jerron brought Jerron before the child.

And Jerron touched the child. And the child did not touch Jerron. And Jerron was not healed for God knew the heart of Jerron. And Jerron was not of God and a follower of the Christ. For Jerron cared not for those of misfortune.

And Jerron commanded his servants return him to his place. And the servants returned Jerron to his place.

The Gift of Copper, Silver, and Gold

And Jerron called forth his servants. And Jerron spoke saying, "My gift of food and cloth was not great enough for God. I will send a greater gift."

And Jerron held a chest of coin. And Jerron commanded of the servants, "Take this chest of copper, silver, and gold to the place of Cephus. Present this chest before the child. When God sees my great gift, the child will touch me and I will be healed."

And the servants brought the chest of coin to the place of Cephus. And the servants lay the chest before the child. And Josep spoke saying, "God does not ask for copper, silver, or gold."

And the chest was given to Ahel. And Josep asked the coins be given to those of misfortune. And Ahel went outside the place of Cephus. And Ahel handed the coins to those who waited.

And there was a young boy among those who waited. And the young boy was a cripple. And the young boy carried a crutch made from the branch of the olive tree.

And Ahel handed a coin of silver to the young boy. And the young spoke saying, "My needs are small. There is one whose needs are greater. Give my coin to another."

And Ahel gave the silver coin to another. And the coins of copper, silver, and gold were given to those of misfortune.

And the servants of Jerron witnessed the coins given to others. And the servants returned to Jerron. And when the servants returned to Jerron, the day was ended.

And the sun rose.

And Jerron commanded his servants take him to the place of Cephus. And the servants lifted his bed and carried him to the place of Cephus.

And the doors of the home of Cephus are closed. And many waited before the door. For the door would be opened that all may enter and ask God's blessing.

And Jerron was the last. And Jerron commanded his servants take him to the door. And the servants brought Jerron to the door and Jerron was the first.

And the doors were opened. And Cephus commanded of all, "Come into my home. Seek the blessing of God."

And Jerron was the first. And the servants of Jerron brought Jerron before the child.

And Jerron touched the child. And the child did not touch Jerron. And Jerron was not healed for God knew the heart of Jerron. And Jerron was not of God and a follower of the Christ. For Jerron cared not for those of misfortune.

And Jerron commanded his servants return him to his place. And the servants returned Jerron to his place.

The Greatest Gift

And Jerron called forth his servants. And he spoke to them saying, "My wealth is but metal and soil. And I fear the thief who will take my metal and soil. The wealth of God knows no limit and no thief can steal that which God gives. Three times I touched the child and three times the child touched me not. Two times I sent gifts to the child and two times the gifts were given to those of misfortune. "

God knows my heart. And my heart is not of God. I am not a follower of the Christ for I care not for those of misfortune."

And Jerron freed his servants. And he divided his wealth among them. And Jerron sent cloth, food, and coin to those of misfortune.

And Jerron prayed to God to enter his heart.

And God entered the heart of Jerron.

And the sun rose.

God Heals Jerron

And the freed servants came to Jerron. And one spoke saying, "You have given God the greatest gift. We will take you to the place of Cephus. There you will ask God for his blessing."

And the freed servants took up the bed of Jerron. And the freed servants brought gifts of food, cloth, and coin. And the freed servants carried Jerron to the place of Cephus.

And the doors of the home of Cephus are closed. And none waited before the door. For the door would be opened that all may enter and ask God's blessing. And the freed servants of Jerron brought Jerron to the door.

And Jerron was the first. And many came to the place of Cephus. And Jerron asked the freed servants to move his bed back. And Jerron became the last.

And the freed servants gave food, cloth, and coin to those who waited.

And the doors were opened. And Cephus commanded of all, "Come into my home. Seek the blessing of God."

And many went into the place of Cephus to ask God's blessing. And many came to the place of Cephus. And Jerron was not the last. And Jerron asked the freed servants to move his bed back. And Jerron became the last.

And the freed servants gave food, cloth, and coin to those who came.

And Jerron was the last. And the freed servants brought the bed of Jerron unto the place of Cephus. And the freed servants lay the bed of Cephus before the child.

And Jerron spoke to Josep, Mira, and the child saying, "God has entered my heart. My wealth was of man. I seek the wealth of God. For the wealth of man is but metal and soil. The wealth of God is through his promise of eternal life through the teachings of the Christ. For all who believe in the Christ and follow the Christ will enter the kingdom of God. Though I die, I live."

And the child went to the bed of Jerron. And the child lay in the arms of Jerron.

And God healed Jerron through the hands of the child. For God knew the heart of Jerron. And Jerron was of God and a follower of the Christ.

And Jerron returned to his place and he called forth the freed servants. And Jerron spoke saying, "God has entered my heart. I leave this place to speak the teachings of God and the Christ."

And Jerron took up his belongings and he left his place. And the freed servants went with Jerron.

Jerron Draws Water

And Jerron traveled within Hebron. And Jerron spoke of God and the teachings of the Christ. And Jerron spoke to all who would listen. And many came unto God and the Christ from Jerron's words.

And Jerron and the freed servants traveled from Hebron.

And Jerron and the freed servants thirst for water. And they stopped at a small home.

And Jerron knocked on the door of the small home. And a woman with infant child opened the door.

And Jerron asked if he might drink water. And the woman responded, "There is no water in the jar. If there was water in the jar, I would pour water for you."

And Jerron asked, "Where do you draw water?"

And the woman responded, "There is a small stream far from here. It is from this stream that I draw water. I am unable to travel to the stream for my son is young and I have no one to care for him."

And Jerron spoke saying, "Hand to me the jar and I will draw water."

And the woman handed to Jerron a small water jar. And Jerron took the small water jar and the large water jar. And Jerron went to the stream to draw water. And the freed servants took up many jars. And the freed servants went with Jerron to draw water.

And Jerron and the freed servants drew water from the stream. And they carried the water to the place of the woman.

And the woman poured water for Jerron and the freed servants. And they drank the water. And the water was cool to the touch and the water was sweet in its taste.

And Jerron asked the woman if she had food to share. And the woman spoke saying, "I have no food to share. What little I possessed, has been eaten. If I had food, I would share that which I have."

And Jerron asked, "Where do you get food?"

And the woman responded, "I purchase food in the city and food is grown in the field. I have no money to purchase food in the city. No food grows in the field for my husband has not completed plowing and planting the field."

And Jerron asked, "Where is your husband?"

And the woman responded, "My husband spoke against the tax collector. The soldiers of the tax collector took my husband many days ago. I know not the place of my husband."

And Jerron spoke saying, "I once held great wealth and power. If I held my wealth and power, I would set free your husband."

"I have given away my wealth to follow God and the teachings of the Christ. I will give to you that which I can give."

Jerron Plows the Field

And Jerron looked at the field and the plow was set upon the earth. And the field was not complete.

And Jerron sent several to the city to purchase food for the woman. And Jerron went to the field. And Jerron began to plow the field.

And the freed servants went to the field with Jerron. And the men plowed the field and the men planted the seed.

And the freed servants brought food from the city. And the freed servants brought oil for cooking. And Jerron exchanged the promise of the seed for food. And jars were filled with water. And jars were filled with oil. And food was placed in the home. And the woman and child would not hunger or thirst.

And the woman prepared bread. And she gave bread to Jerron and the freed servants. And the bread was hot to the touch and sweet to the taste. And the woman poured water for Jerron and the freed servants. And the water was cool to the touch and sweet to the taste.

And Jerron and the freed servants were to leave. And Jerron spoke, "We leave to speak the words of God and his son Jesus Christ. If we come this way, we will stop and give to you that which we can give."

And a shout was heard. And a man ran to the home.

And the man was named Jest. And the woman was named Sarah. And the infant child was named Jessie.

And Jest came into the home. And he held Sarah and Jessie. And Jest spoke that God sent his angel to deliver him. And Jest spoke of his release.

The Angel of God Delivers Jest

"There were ten and two of us. And we were bound with rope that we could not flee. We were to be taken to Pilate that we would be judged. And we feared the sentence would be death."

"And the sun was setting. And the fires of the camp were lit. And the guards brought bread for food."

"And soldiers came to us. And a soldier spoke of a soldier who rode into camp. And the soldier who rode into camp commanded that the officer be brought before him. And the officer came to him. And the soldier commanded that the prisoners be assembled before him. And the officer ordered that the prisoners be brought forth."

"And the soldiers took us before the soldier who rode into camp."

"And the soldier was unlike any I have seen. And the soldier was large. And the color of his horse was white like the cloud."

"And the soldier wore a breast plate of gold and silver. And upon his head was a helmet of gold and silver. And his hair was of dark black and his beard was of dark black. And his eyes were as fire."

"And his saddle shone like the sun. And the bridle of his horse was of leather I have not seen."

"And the hilt of his sword was of gold. And the soldier carried no shield."

"And we were assembled before the soldier. And the soldier dismounted his horse."

"And we lowered our heads before the soldier. And the soldier walked among us. And the soldier stopped before one of the twelve."

"And the soldier spoke to the man saying, 'What is your name?'"

"And the man answered, 'My name is Evan.'"

"And the soldier spoke saying,' Your son Jacob is great with courage."

"Of your son, God is pleased."

"And the soldier spoke saying, 'I have been sent by God to deliver you."

"And the soldier returned to his horse and the soldier mounted his horse."

"And the soldier commanded of the officer saying, 'Has any man taken sword against Caesar or Rome?"

"The officer answered, 'No man has taken sword against Caesar or Rome."

"The soldier commanded, 'Why are these men held captive?"

"The officer answered, 'These men spoke against the tax collector."

"The soldier commanded, 'What words were spoken?"

"The officer answered, 'These men spoke that they could not pay the tax for to pay the tax would leave their families hungry for food. These men did not pay the tax."

"The soldier commanded, 'Where do you take these men?"

"The officer answered, 'These men are to be taken before Pilate that Pilate may judge them."

"The soldier commanded, 'Pilate need not judge these men. God judged these men. These men did not seek to raise sword against Caesar or Rome. These men sought to protect their families and their homes."

"Of these men, God is pleased."

"Bring food and water to each man that he may not hunger or thirst on his journey home."

"And the soldier commanded, 'Free these men!"

"The officer asked, 'Who orders their release?"

"And the soldier drew his sword from its sheath. And the sword was of silver and gold. And the sword burned with white fire. And the fire covered the soldier. And the fire covered his horse. And the sword, soldier, and horse burned in white fire."

"And the soldier held the sword of white fire in air and the soldier commanded saying, 'No man orders their release!"

"God commands these men set free!"

"And we trembled and fell to our knees. For before us was not a soldier of Caesar. Before us was the angel of God."

"And many soldiers released their weapons and ran from the camp. And the officer ordered that our ropes be untied to set us free. And the officer ordered rations of food and water to be given to each man. And the soldiers hurried to untie our ropes and those ropes that could not be untied were cut by the knife of the soldier."

"And each man was untied. And each man ran from the camp, as he was untied. And I ran from the camp when my ropes were untied. And the ten and two of us were set free. And we ran from the camp."

"And the angel of God moved his horse before the soldiers. And the angel of God held his sword of white fire in air that no soldier would follow."

"And no soldier could defeat the angel of God. And no army could defeat the angel of God. For the angel of God and his horse burned with the fire of God. And the fire of God did not consume the angel and his horse. For the angel of God commanded the fire of God."

"And no soldier raised his sword in battle. And no soldier followed. And no soldier was harmed. For the soldiers obeyed the command of God."

"And the soldiers ran from the camp. And the camp was barren."

"And I witnessed the angel of God return his sword to its sheath. And the white fire left the angel of God and his horse. And I witnessed the angel of God ride his horse from the camp."

"And we ran from the camp. And ten and one of us gathered at the edge of the wood. And we marveled at what had occurred."

"And we talked among ourselves of the angel who had knowledge of the man Evan. And we talked among ourselves of the angel who had knowledge of the son of Evan."

"And we knew not the man Evan or his son Jacob."

"And we thanked God for his blessing. For the angel of God delivered us."

"And we vowed to find Evan and his son. And we vowed to guard and protect those who could not protect themselves. And we vowed to return to our families to provide food."

"When our families are provided, we will meet."

"And I ran home thanking God for his blessing."

Many Work as One

And Jest marveled at the jars of water and oil. And Jest marveled at the field that was complete. And Jest marveled at the food.

And Jest thanked Jerron and all those who helped his family.

And Jerron spoke saying, "I held great wealth and power. Of these men I have knowledge. Of these men I know their law."

"We will work together. If the many work as one, there is no task we can not complete."

And Jest knew the place of one of the twelve.

And they left the place of Jest to journey to the place of one of the twelve.

And they came to the place of one of the twelve. And the man was named Abram. And Abram plowed the field. And the field was not complete.

And the water jars were empty. And there was no food. And the wife of Abram was named Celene. And Celene was with child.

And the many took up the jars. And the many drew water. And the many went to the field. And Jerron and the many plowed the field. And Jerron and the many planted seed.

And the many went to the city. And Jerron exchanged the promise of the seed for food. And jars were filled with water. And jars were filled with oil. And food was placed in the home.

And the many worked as one. And the tasks were complete.

And Celene prepared bread for food. And she poured water to drink. And the bread was hot to the touch and sweet in taste. And the water was cool to the touch and sweet in taste.

And Abram knew the place of one of the twelve.

And they left the place of Abram to journey to the place of one of the twelve.

רבקה
Jerron Speaks the Law

And they came to the place of one of the twelve. And the tax collector was at his place. And there were many soldiers with the tax collector.

And Jerron went to the tax collector. And Jerron spoke to the tax collector. And Jerron spoke the law of Caesar. And Jerron spoke the law of Rome. And Jerron spoke the names of men of great power of whom he had knowledge.

And the tax collector feared Jerron. For Jerron knew of the law and men of great power.

And the tax collector and his soldiers left the place of one of the twelve.

And the name of one of the twelve was John. And John thanked the many.

And the many worked as one. And the jars of water were filled. And the field was plowed and seed planted. And Jerron exchanged the promise of the seed for food. And food and oil was brought unto the place of John. And the tasks were complete.

The Eleven Gather Together

And John knew the place of one of the twelve. And the many traveled to the place of one of the twelve. And the many worked as one. And the tasks were complete.

And the many traveled to the place of the others of the eleven. And the many worked as one. And the tasks were complete.

And all the tasks were complete. And the eleven gathered together.

And the eleven vowed to guard and protect those who could not protect themselves. And the eleven vowed to help those harmed by the tax collector.

And Jerron spoke the word of God to the eleven. And Jerron spoke the teachings of the Christ. And the eleven came unto God and the Christ.

רבקה

The Freed Servants Leave Jerron

And the freed servants came before Jerron. And one spoke saying, "We worked as servants before you and we feared you. For you held great wealth and power."

"You gave up your wealth and power to follow God and the teachings of the Christ. You gave us our freedom. You divided your wealth among us. And we gave up our wealth as you gave up your wealth."

"God healed you and God blessed you. And God has blessed us. We have traveled many places with you."

"We have heard your words of God and the Christ and we know your words."

"We will leave you. We leave to share your words of God and the Christ. We will speak as many, we will speak as one."

And Jerron spoke saying, "I stay with these men for my work is not complete."

And the freed servants left Jerron and the eleven. And the freed servants spoke the word of God and the Christ. And many came unto God and the Christ from their words.

The Search for Evan and Jacob

And the twelve traveled in search of Evan and the son of Evan named Jacob. And the twelve traveled as one. And the twelve worked as one. And there was no task, which they could not complete.

God Delivers Hebron

The Many Work As One

And the twelve traveled in search of Evan and his son Jacob.

And they came to the place of Evan. And Evan and his son plowed the field. And the field was not complete. And the water jars were empty. And there was no food.

And Jerron came to Evan. And Jerron spoke of God's blessing to him. And Jerron spoke of the eleven. And Evan knew of the eleven. For the angel of God delivered the twelve.

And the eleven told Evan of their vow to guard and protect those who cannot protect themselves. And Evan and his son took the vow.

And the many worked as one. And the field was complete. And seed was planted. And Jerron exchanged the promise of the seed for food. And food and oil were brought unto the place of Evan. And the tasks were complete.

And the eleven vowed to return to collect the harvest. And they thanked God for their blessings. And the eleven returned to their homes. And Jerron stayed at the place of Evan.

And time passed. And the seed grew strong and plentiful. And the eleven returned to the place of Evan to gather the harvest.

And the eleven brought with them their wives and their children.

And the many worked as one. And the men gathered the harvest and the women and children prepared the grain.

And the tasks were complete.

And the many gave thanks to God. And Jerron spoke the word of God and the teachings of the Christ.

The Harvest is Divided

And Jerron spoke to the many saying, "God has blessed us for the seed gave great harvest. We will divide the harvest into two."

"One of the two we will return the promise of the seed. That which remains will be sold at fair price. From this fair price we will purchase food and hold to those coins not exchanged for food."

"The two we will give to those of misfortune."

And the harvest was divided into two. And the many took the one to return the promise of the seed. And Jerron sold that which remained at fair price. And they purchased food with the coin. And they held to the coin, which remained

And the two was given to those of misfortune.

And the many went to the place of one of the eleven. And Evan, Elizabeth, and Jacob went with the many.

And the many worked as one. And the men gathered the harvest and the women and children prepared the grain.

And the tasks were complete.

And the many gave thanks to God. And Jerron spoke the word of God and the teachings of the Christ.

And the harvest was divided into two. And the many took the one to return the promise of the seed. And Jerron sold that which remained at fair price. And they purchased food with the coin. And they held to the coin that remained.

And the coin that remained was placed with the coin, which remained from the harvest of Evan.

And the two was given to those of misfortune.

And the many went to the place of one of the eleven. And the many worked as one.

And the harvest was gathered from the fields of the twelve. And the harvest was divided into two from each of the twelve fields. And one of the two returned the promise of the seed. And Jerron sold that which remained at fair price. And food was purchased with the coin. And they held to the coin that remained.

And the coin that remained of the two was joined together.

And the two of the twelve harvests were given to those of misfortune.

And the many worked as one. And the many helped those of misfortune. And the coin that was joined was used to pay the tax of those whom could not pay the tax.

And the planting came before the harvest. And the harvest came before the planting.

And the many worked as one to complete the planting. And God blessed the seed. And the harvest of the seed was great. And the many worked as one to gather the harvest.

And the harvest was divided into two. And one of the two returned the promise of the seed. And Jerron sold that which remained at fair price. And food was purchased with the coin. And they held to the coin that remained.

And the coin that remained of the two was joined together.

And the two of the twelve harvests were given to those of misfortune.

And the coin that was joined was used to pay the tax of those who could not pay the tax.

And the seasons passed. And each harvest was great.

And Jacob grew in age. And the boy grew into a man.

And Jerron spoke the word of God and the teachings of the Christ. And the people came unto God and the Christ.

And the many built a temple to God and the Christ. And Jerron was the keeper of the temple. And Jerron was the keeper of the word of God and the teachings of the Christ. And many came to the temple to hear Jerron speak the word of God and the teachings of the Christ. And many came unto God and the Christ from his words.

And the soldiers of the tax collector did no harm to the people. And there was peace in Hebron.

And the tax collector was summoned to Rome. And he was gone for many months. And a tax collector was sent to Hebron. And the tax collector was not the one before.

And the tax collector collected more tax than ordered by Rome. And the tax collector built a great place with the tax. And the tax collector increased his soldiers.

And the tax collector built a prison with the tax. And the prison was the place of the soldiers. And the prison held many rooms with doors of iron joined to stone. And the prison held a great arena. And the soldiers battled for pleasure in the arena. And the soldiers practiced their skills of battle in the arena.

And the tax collector sent his soldiers to collect the tax. And those men who could not pay the tax were brought to the arena.

And the soldiers battled these men for pleasure. And the tax collector watched the battles.

Jacob Battles the Soldiers

And Jacob walked on the road and he carried food to give to one of misfortune. And Jacob carried no weapon. And the soldiers of the tax collector came upon him.

And the soldiers were armed with sword and shield. And the soldiers were many and Jacob was one. And the soldiers took Jacob. And Jacob was brought to the prison.

And Jacob was placed in a room of stone. And the door was of iron joined to stone.

And word of Jacob's arrest came to Evan and Jerron. And Evan and Jerron went to the tax collector. And Jerron spoke to the tax collector. And Jerron spoke the law of Caesar. And Jerron spoke the law of Rome. And the tax collector did not hear his words. And Jerron spoke the names of men of great power of whom he had knowledge. And the tax collector did not hear their names.

And Jerron gave coin to the tax collector. And the tax collector took the coin.

And the tax collector spoke saying, "This man will battle my soldiers. If he wins, I will set him free. If he loses, I will give him to you."

And the tax collector dismissed Evan and Jerron. And Evan and Jerron were sent from the prison.

And Jacob was brought unto the arena. And there were many soldiers.

And before him stood six soldiers. And the soldiers held sword and shield. And Jacob held no weapon.

And the tax collector spoke saying, "If you defeat these men. I will set you free."

And Jacob spoke saying, "I have no weapon to defend myself."

And the tax collector spoke saying, "Give him a sword."

And a soldier pulled his sword from its sheath and he threw the sword to Jacob's feet.

And Jacob spoke saying, "I have no shield."

And the tax collector spoke saying, "You ask too much."

And the tax collector sat in his chair. And he raised his hand for battle to begin.

And the sword lay at Jacob's feet. And the six soldiers moved before Jacob. And the six soldiers were armed with sword and shield.

And Jacob had not held a sword. And Jacob looked at the six soldiers. And the six soldiers moved before Jacob.

And Jacob heard a voice.

And the voice was from a time long past. The voice he heard was of Josep.

And the voice of Josep said, 'You battled these men with a crutch of wood and your leg is twisted. How did you hope to defeat these men in battle?"

And Jacob heard his own voice respond.

'I asked God for strength to battle these three men. I asked God to give me strength that I may free the child. I battled to save the child. My leg is of no concern."

And Jacob heard the voice of Ahel.

And the voice of Ahel said, 'I have not witnessed such skill in battle. No man has torn the shield from my arm."

And Jacob heard the voice of Mahal.

And the voice of Mahal said, 'No man has struck such blows."

And Jacob heard the voice of Jaykal.

And the voice of Jaykal said, 'My brothers speak truth. I have not witnessed such skill in battle. No man has struck such blows."

"You believed the child was at arrest and you risked your life to save the child. You are a great warrior. If you battled with sword, truly you would defeat us."

And Jacob knew his strength and his skill came from God.

And Jacob took up the sword.

And one soldier ran to Jacob. And Jacob struck the shield of the soldier with a great blow. And the blow tore the shield from the arm of the soldier. And Jacob struck the soldier with the hilt of the sword. And the soldier fell to ground.

And the soldiers who witnessed this event were alarmed.

And the tax collector waved his hand for the soldiers to stand.

And five soldiers moved before Jacob.

And one soldier ran to Jacob. And Jacob struck the shield of the soldier with a great blow. And the blow tore the shield from the arm of the soldier. And Jacob struck the soldier with the hilt of the sword. And the soldier fell to ground.

And the soldiers who witnessed this event moved toward Jacob.

And the tax collector waved his hand for the soldiers to move back.

And four soldiers moved before Jacob and two soldiers lay to ground.

And Jacob went to the first soldier he battled and Jacob took up his sword.

And Jacob held two swords. And one sword he held in his left hand and one sword he held in his right hand.

And two soldiers ran to Jacob. And Jacob struck the shield of one soldier with the sword in his left hand. And the blow tore the shield from the arm of the soldier. And Jacob struck the shield of the second soldier with both swords. And the blow pierced the shield and the blow pierced the soldier. And the soldier fell to ground dead from the blow.

And Jacob struck the first soldier with the hilt of the sword in his right hand and the soldier fell to ground.

And the soldiers who witnessed these events moved toward Jacob.

And the tax collector waved his hand for the soldiers to stand.

And the tax collector spoke saying, "Two more."

And the two soldiers looked at the four who lay to ground. And one soldier lay dead from the blow. And the two soldiers looked at the shield pierced by the two swords.

And Jacob stood before them with two swords. One sword he held in his left hand and one sword he held in his right hand.

And the two soldiers released their swords and their shields. And the two soldiers ran from Jacob.

And the tax collector spoke saying, "The sword you hold defeated the six. I have a need for you. Come unto my will and I will give you power and wealth."

And Jacob spoke saying, "I follow the will of another."

And the tax collector spoke saying, "Are you a Christian?"

And Jacob spoke saying, "I know not of the word."

And the tax collector spoke saying, "Do you follow God and the teachings of the Christ?"

And Jacob spoke saying, "Yes. I follow God and the Christ."

And the tax collector spoke saying, "A waste."

"What is your name?"

And Jacob spoke saying, "My name is Jacob. I am the son of Evan and Elizabeth."

And the tax collector spoke saying, "You are free to go. The sword you hold defeated the six."

"I will see you again."

And Jacob released the swords. And Jacob was sent from the prison.

And a soldier came to the tax collector. And the soldier spoke saying, "Why did you release this man? There are many who wish to battle him."

And the tax collector spoke saying, "The sword he held defeated the six."

And the soldier spoke saying, "The sword he held defeated only four. Two ran from him."

And the tax collector commanded, "Bring the two to me."

And the two were brought before the tax collector. And the tax collector commanded, "Bring me the sword held by Jacob."

And the sword held by Jacob was handed to the tax collector. And the tax collector took the sword held by Jacob and he killed the two.

And the tax collector threw the sword to ground. And the tax collector spoke saying, "The sword held by Jacob defeated the six."

And Jacob went to the temple of God. And Jacob asked God's forgiveness, for he killed a man.

And Jerron came to Jacob. And Jerron spoke to Jacob saying, "It was not by your will you killed this man. You battled to save yourself. God gave you strength and skill to defeat these men. Of these gifts, you will do God's will."

And Jacob returned to his place.

The Thirteen Protect the People

And word of Jacob's battle came to the eleven. And the eleven came to the place of Evan. And the thirteen took up swords that they may protect those who could not protect themselves.

And the soldiers of the tax collector were cruel to the people. And many were taken to the prison of the soldiers.

And Jerron spoke to the tax collector. And Jerron spoke the law of Caesar and Rome. And the tax collector did not hear his words. And Jerron gave coin to the tax collector for the tax. And the tax collector took the coin. And the men were not released.

And Evan, Jacob, and the eleven battled the soldiers to protect the people. And the soldiers took men prisoner. And Evan, Jacob, and the eleven freed the men.

And Evan, Jacob, and the eleven were everywhere. And Evan, Jacob, and the eleven were nowhere.

And the soldiers feared battle with Jacob. For Jacob commanded the sword. No man was his equal. And Jacob defeated all whom he battled.

And the tax collector increased his soldiers. And the soldiers brought great suffering to the people of Hebron.

And Evan, Jacob, and the eleven battled the soldiers to protect those who could not protect themselves.

And Jerron spoke to the tax collector. And Jerron spoke the law of Caesar and Rome. And the tax collector did not hear his words. And Jerron gave coin to the tax collector for the tax. And the tax collector took the coin. And the men were not released.

And the soldiers of the tax collector feared battle with Evan, Jacob, and the eleven. And the soldiers feared to collect the tax. For many soldiers were defeated by Jacob.

And the tax collector plotted to capture Evan, Jacob, and the eleven.

The Plot of the Tax Collector

And the soldiers of the tax collector were sent to arrest one man. And the soldiers bound the man with rope. And the soldiers held the man's wife and their child.

And Evan, Jacob, and the eleven came to the place of the man. And the man was bound with rope and the soldiers held the man's wife and child.

And Evan, Jacob, and the eleven stood to battle. And the soldier who held the child held his sword to the child.

And the soldier who held the child commanded, "Release your weapons and come unto my will or I murder the child!"

And Evan spoke saying, "You will not murder this child. For we will defeat you."

And the soldier who held the child commanded, "There are many soldiers and many children. If you defeat us, many children will die."

And the soldier cut the leg of the child with his sword.

And Jacob spoke saying, "If we release our weapons and come unto your will, will you not harm the child?"

And the soldier who held the child spoke saying, "The tax collector commands his soldiers to murder children if you do not release your weapons and come unto my will. If you do these things, we are ordered not to harm this child or any child."

And Evan, Jacob, and the eleven released their weapons. And the soldiers released the man, his wife, and the child.

And Evan, Jacob, and the eleven were bound with rope. And they were taken to the prison of the soldiers.

And Evan, Jacob, and the eleven were placed in a great room. And the room was of stone. And the door of the room was of iron joined to the stone.

And the soldiers gathered in the arena. And the tax collector came to the arena to witness the battle. And the tax collector brought many with him to witness the battle.

And each man was to be brought unto the arena to battle. And each man would hold no weapon. And Evan was first to battle. And Jacob was last to battle.

And the soldiers prepared their arrows. And the soldiers prepared their spears. And the soldiers took up their swords and shields.

And Jerron heard of the capture of the thirteen. And Jerron went to the temple of God to pray. And Jerron prayed to God to save the men.

The Angel of God Delivers the Thirteen

And the thirteen men struggled to free the iron door from its stone. And the door of iron would not move. And the door of iron held to its stone.

And the men heard a voice. The voice came from behind them.

And the voice said, "No man can open this door. Only the power of God can open this door."

And the thirteen men turned to see a soldier in the room with them. And the soldier wore a breastplate of gold and silver. And upon his head was a helmet of gold and silver. And his hair was of dark black and his beard was of dark black. And his eyes were as fire.

And the hilt of his sword was of gold. And the soldier carried no shield.

And the twelve knew of the soldier. For before them stood the angel of God.

And the thirteen lowered their head before the angel of God.

And Jacob spoke saying, "I know of you."

And the angel of God spoke saying, "My brothers speak truth. I have not witnessed such skill in battle. No man has struck such blows."

And Jacob spoke saying, "Jaykal!"

And the angel of God spoke saying, "It is I, Jaykal."

And the thirteen lowered their heads before the angel Jaykal.

And the angel Jaykal spoke to Jacob saying, "You battled to save a child of God. You released your weapon to save a child of man."

"Of you and these men, God is pleased."

"I have been sent by God to deliver you."

"I have been sent by God to deliver Hebron."

And the angel Jaykal walked to the door of iron. And he neared the door. And he raised his hand before the door. And the door of iron tore from its stone.

And the angel Jaykal walked through the opened door. And the angel Jaykal walked toward the arena.

And the thirteen men followed the angel Jaykal. And the angel Jaykal moved with great speed. And the thirteen men ran after him.

And the angel Jaykal came to the opening to the arena. And he turned and held up his hand to bar their path.

And the angel Jaykal spoke saying, "This is not your battle. God judged these men. I deliver the judgment of God."

And the angel Jaykal walked into the arena.

The Angel of God Delivers Hebron

And the soldiers were alarmed at the soldier before them. For the soldier wore a breastplate of gold and silver. And his helmet was of gold and silver. And the hilt of his sword was of gold. And the soldier carried no shield.

And the tax collector was afraid of this soldier. And the hand of the tax collector shook with fear.

And the soldiers looked to the tax collector for his command.

And water was on the forehead of the tax collector. And his face showed great fear. And his hands shook with fear.

And the tax collector gave no command.

And the soldiers readied their arrows. And the soldiers readied their spears. And the soldiers drew their swords and held their shields.

And the angel Jaykal drew his sword from its sheath. And the sword was of silver and gold. And the sword burned with white fire. And the white fire covered the angel Jaykal.

And the tax collector yelled a scream of terror. For before him stood the angel of God.

And no soldier could defeat the angel of God. And no army could defeat the angel of God. For the angel of God burned with the fire of God. And the fire of God did not consume the angel. For the angel of God commanded the fire of God.

And the angel Jaykal held his sword of white fire in air and the angel Jaykal commanded saying, "I deliver the judgment of God!"

And the soldiers released their arrows. And the soldiers threw their spears. And the soldiers charged with sword and shield.

And the angel Jaykal went before the soldiers as a great wind before grains of sand.

And the fire of God consumed the soldier who released the arrow. And the fire of God consumed the soldier who threw the spear. And the fire of God consumed the soldier with sword and shield. And the fire of God consumed the tax collector and those who stood with him.

The fire of God consumed all.

And the thirteen witnessed the angel Jaykal return his sword to its sheath. And the white fire left the angel Jaykal.

And the angel Jaykal spoke saying, "The people of Hebron are free. This is the will of God."

And the angel Jaykal became as a shadow before them.

And no soldier was in the prison. And no soldier guarded those who were imprisoned. For all the soldiers were consumed. And the thirteen released those who were imprisoned.

And the many went from the prison to the temple of God. And the many thanked God for his blessing.

And Jerron spoke to the many saying, "We follow the word of God. We follow the teachings of the Christ. We give ourselves to God and the Christ. The blessings of God have no end. Christ redeems all."

Hebron is at Peace

And the city of Hebron was without a tax collector for many months. And a tax collector was sent to Hebron from Rome.

And the tax collector summed Jerron before him. And the tax collector spoke saying, "I have been sent from Rome to collect the tax. I have been given power to make all judgments on those who can not pay the tax."

"The tax will be fair. No harm will come to those who cannot pay the tax. We will work together."

And the seed of the harvest was great. And the many worked as one. And each harvest was divided into two. And the two of the two was given to those of misfortune. And the coin from the fair sale of the one was joined together. And Jerron was the keeper of the coin.

And the tax collector collected no more tax than was due. And the tax was fair. And no harm came to those who could not pay the tax. And of those who could not pay the tax, Jerron paid their tax from the coins of the harvest.

And Evan, Jacob, and the eleven laid down their swords. For the people of Hebron were at peace.

רבקה

The Judging of Nafta, Brema, and Salan

Prologue to The Judging of Nafta, Brema, and Salan

In the desert of Syria lies a Mosque. This Mosque contains many scrolls written at the time of Christ. The scrolls record the events of the area and the scrolls record the many tribes who lived in the desert.

One scroll records an event that occurred many years after the crucifixion of Jesus Christ. The event concerns a young child healed by God and blessed by God. God healed through the hands of the child.

The specific event recorded on this scroll is the trial of a thief. The thief sought to murder a child for a silver coin. An elder chief gave the silver coin to the child.

The elder chief's daughter had been ill and God healed the chief's daughter through the hands of the child. The silver coin was a gift of thanks to God and the child.

The thief attempted to steal the coin and during the theft guards captured him. The scroll records the trial of the thief and the scroll records events that occurred before the trial.

The scroll is titled - The Judging of Nafta, Brema, and Salan

The Judging of Nafta, Brema, and Salan

There comes before the elder chiefs a thief named Nafta. Nafta is accused of plotting to kill a child to take a silver coin. Nafta is accused of having two with him. The two are Brema and Salan.

Rasha gave the silver coin to the child Aaron. The gift was a gesture of thanks to God.

Nafta, Brema, and Salan plotted to murder the child for the silver coin. Brema and Salan have fled.

Nasa, Kashin, and Mahad will judge Nafta. If Nafta, Brema, and Salan are judged guilty, the penalty is death.

Placed before the judges is a chain of gold with a silver coin attached.

Rasha's words -

"My daughter Alena became very ill. She had the fever, which killed seven of our tribe. The last of the fever is but two moons. Word came of a child healed by God and blessed by God. God heals through the touch of the child."

"The child was spoken near the oasis of Shimra. And the oasis is but one moon before and after. Several of my tribesmen went to seek the child. The child was found and brought to Alena."

"Alena was near death and the child touch her. The fever left her and Alena was well."

"I offered my tent to the child and the child's parents. Alena was well and she tended the child. One other had the fever. The child touched them and the fever left."

"The child sits with his parents. The child is named Aaron. Aaron was once ill with fever and God healed Aaron through the touch of a child. Aaron was given the gift to heal from the child and God heals through the hands of Aaron."

"Aaron is blessed by God."

"I prayed to God for his blessing and I brought this gift to the child. The gift is a chain of gold. Attached to the chain is a silver coin. The coin is the silver coin shown to Jesus Christ by the Pharisees. The coin bears the image of Caesar."

"The coin is my possession. I purchased the coin from a Pharisee and my craftsman prepared the gold chain and attached the coin. The coin is a reminder to give to God what God asks."

"My gift was accepted and I placed the chain of gold around the neck of the child. For the child is of God and the coin was in the presence of God's son, Jesus Christ."

"I was told three men attempted to murder the child for the coin. Two of the three have fled. One man, Nafta, was captured in my tent. In his hand he held a knife. He confessed he and two others sought to murder the child for the coin."

Jaka's words -

"I am a guard of Rasha. I was alerted to sounds in Rasha's tent. I entered the tent and I found the man Nafta with a knife. I struggled with Nafta and I loosened the knife."

"Nafta spoke that two men, Brema and Salan, had entered the tent before him. The tent was searched but the two men were not found. The child with parents and Alena were the only ones in the tent. The tent has no tear."

"Nafta spoke that three plotted to murder the child for the gold chain and silver coin. Brema and Salan have fled. Guards search the desert for Brema and Salan."

Alena's words -

"I was ill with fever and my father heard of the child Aaron. And Aaron was at the oasis of Shimra. The child was brought to me. I touched Aaron and Aaron touched me. God healed me."

"I gave care to the child and the child and I were together. We slept in my father's tent. I was awakened by a struggle. Jaka held a man in the tent. The man was Nafta."

"Nafta confessed that he sought to murder the child to steal the necklace and coin. Nafta spoke that Brema and Salan entered the tent. I heard and witnessed only Nafta. I heard or witnessed no other."

Mikal's words -

"My son was very ill with fever. We heard of a child healed by God and blessed by God. God healed through the hands of the child. We traveled to Tiberias in search of the child."

"We stopped at a well near Tiberias to cool our son with water. At the well was the young girl Rebecca. God healed our son Aaron through Rebecca's hands and the gift given to Rebecca was given to Aaron. God heals through the hands of Aaron."

"Rebecca spoke that it is the will of God that generations to come will know the power of God through the hands of a child. What was given to her was taken from her. What was taken from her was given to Aaron. God himself protects Aaron. No man, woman, child, or beast of the earth shall harm our son. This is the will of God."

"Aaron is blessed by God for God has healed many through the hands of Aaron."

"We were at the oasis of Shimra. Rasha asked that we travel to his camp. God healed Alena through the hands of Aaron."

"We slept in the tent of Rasha. We were awakened when Jaka struggled with Nafta. Nafta spoke of two men who entered the tent. I only witnessed Nafta."

Nafta's words -

"Brema and Salan plotted to steal the gold and silver the child wore. We witnessed Rasha give the gift to the child. The gold and silver are very valuable to the correct buyer."

"We waited for everyone to sleep. Jaka walked from tent to tent. We waited for Jaka to walk from the tent. Brema was to enter the tent and murder the child. He would bring the gold and silver to Salan. We planned to travel to the oasis of Shimra. We would sell the gold and silver."

"Brema entered the tent. We waited for Brema. Brema did not leave the tent. We heard no alarm. Salan feared Brema had murdered the child and taken the gold and silver."

"Salan entered the tent. I waited for Brema and Salan. They did not leave the tent. I heard no alarm. I feared that they had murdered the child and taken the gold and silver."

"I entered the tent. Near the tent was a vessel. The vessel overturned and Jaka came to me. We struggled."

"Brema and Salan entered the tent. They did not leave. The child wore the gold and silver around his neck. Brema and Salan fled to the desert."

"I am guilty of plotting to steal. There has been no murder. The child sits."

"There has been no theft. The gold and silver lays upon the skin. No harm has come to the child. No harm has come to the gold and silver."

"I am guilty of no crime but ignorance."

Kashin's words -

"There has been no murder. The murder was planned. Jaka stopped the murder when the vessel was struck. The noise alerted Jaka."

"Brema and Salan plotted to murder. They fled to the desert. They will be found and punished."

"There has been no theft. The theft was planned. Three attempted to steal the property of the child and three failed. The child's property lays before us on skin."

"Three wanted the child's property and three planned to murder the child for the property."

"By Nafta's own words he admits to plotting murder and theft. By Nafta's own words he witnesses against Brema and Salan."

"If not for the sound of a vessel, the child would lay murdered."

"The verdict is guilty for Nafta, Brema, and Salan."

Nasa's words -

"Nafta, Brema, and Salan are guilty."

Mahad's words -

"Nafta, Brema, and Salan are guilty."

Nafta's words -

"Do not kill me! There has been no crime. Have mercy on me."

Mahad's words -

"You have been determined guilty. You will be executed."

Aaron gestures -

Aaron went to the skin where the necklace of gold and the silver coin lay. Aaron picked up the necklace and he went to Nafta.

Nafta lay on the tent floor crying.

Aaron touched the shoulder of Nafta and Aaron placed the necklace in Nafta's hand.

Aaron returned to where he sat beside his father and his mother.

Nafta's words -

"God shows me mercy. The child I sought to murder approached me with no fear. That which I sought to steal has been given to me. God gives his mercy and his forgiveness."

"I thank God that Brema and Salan did not murder the child."

Kashin's words -

"Rasha spoke witness the child is blessed by God. Mikal spoke witness the child is blessed by God. Alena spoke witness God healed her through the hands of the child. I have no doubt this child is blessed by God and God gives his blessing through the hands of the child."

"God is a higher authority than I. God has spoken through the hands of Aaron."

"God has forgiven Nafta and that which he coveted has been handed to him."

"God has spoken. Nafta is free to go."

Nasa's words -

"God has spoken. Nafta is free to go."

Mahad's words -

"God has spoken. Nafta is free to go."

Nafta was set free.

רבקה

Beathag

Agymah sat in his chair trying to get comfortable. He had another illness come to him. This illness was as the others; Agymah went to sleep while he was awake. His body moved and he could not stop the movements. He bit his tongue.

His servant placed a wet cloth in his mouth to hold his tongue. The illness was as the others, frightening.

A guard came into the room of Agymah. The guard bowed.

Agymah spoke, "Why do you disturb me?"

The guard spoke, "I have been sent to you by Apophis. There are three Hebrews who wish to see Manu. Apophis will not allow them to see Manu. The three Hebrews will not leave."

"What are your orders?"

Agymah spoke, "Who are they? Why do they wish to see Manu?"

The guard spoke, "The three are a man, woman, and a young girl. The young girl speaks that the God of the Hebrews sent her to Manu. The God of the Hebrews will heal Manu through her hands."

Agymah spoke, "Is Manu ill?"

The guard spoke, "Manu harmed his leg. The leg is dark in color and smells like dead cattle. Manu has fever. He will die."

Agymah spoke, "Why does the God of the Hebrews wish to heal Manu? I am ill."

The guard did not answer.

Agymah spoke, "Bring them before me."

The guard bowed and he left. Shortly, the guard entered the room with Apophis, a man, a woman, and a young girl. The young girl was but eight years in age.

The young girl spoke to Agymah, "I am Beathag. There are two in your house who are ill. One is a man. Two is a young child. God has sent me to these two. God will heal them through my hands."

Agymah spoke, "Am I the man?"

Beathag spoke, "No. The man whom God will heal is your servant."

Agymah spoke, "Why would the God of the Hebrews heal this man? I am ill."

Beathag spoke, "The man who is ill has many friends. These friends prayed to God to help their friend. God heard their prayers. God has sent me to answer their prayers."

Agymah spoke, "God will heal me?"

Beathag spoke, "God will not heal you through my hands for you are not of God. The man who is ill is of God."

Agymah spoke, "How does God heal through your hands?"

Beathag spoke, "The one asks for God's blessing and the one touches me. If it is God's will, the Holy Ghost comes upon me. The hand of God reaches through my hands and it is the hand of God that heals."

Agymah stood very quickly. He walked to Beathag and he spoke, "I ask for the God of the Hebrews blessing."

Agymah touched Beathag. Beathag did not touch Agymah.

Agymah spoke, "Why do you not touch me?"

Beathag spoke, "God will not heal you for the Holy Ghost did not come upon me."

Agymah laughed. He spoke, "Such things from a little girl. The God of the Hebrews will heal a old servant but he will not heal a man of power and wealth."

Beathag spoke, "You laugh at God."

Agymah spoke, "I will let you see Manu. I will watch your God heal him. If the God of the Hebrews heals Manu, I will worship this God."

רבקה

Agymah paused and he spoke, "You said God sent you to two in this house. If Manu is the man who is the young child?"

Beathag spoke, "There is a infant child of your servant. The child is ill."

Apophis spoke, "There is a child. A young boy but one year of age. He is the child of your servant Dendera. The child is named Muslim. The child became ill only days ago. I do not know how knowledge of the child's illness was sent to this child."

Agymah spoke, "How did you get knowledge of the child of Dendera?"

Beathag spoke, "God spoke to me in prayer. I have been sent by God to this child."

Agymah spoke, "Let us go to the child. I will witness your God heal the child."

Beathag spoke, "No! God will heal the man through my hands. God will heal the child through my hands last."

Agymah spoke, "If it is your God's will to heal the child through your hands last I will not speak of it. We will go to Manu."

Apophis turned and he requested they follow him. They walked from the house to the area of servants. The area was far from the house and there were many small houses. The houses were made of brick and there were many smells.

There were kettles of soup before the houses and the soup was made from scraps of food. The food had the smell of spoiled meat and vegetables.

They came to a small house and there were many people there. The people knew Apophis and Agymah. The people knew the guard. The people did not know the young Hebrew girl or the Hebrew man and woman.

The people quickly left the house. The people were afraid of the guard and Apophis.

Beathag entered the small house first. Agymah followed her. Within the small house was a bed of cloth. Manu lay upon the bed. His leg was black and the house smelled like dead animals. Apophis gagged from the smell. Agymah held his hand before his face.

Beathag spoke to Agymah and Apophis, "This man has many friends for he is a good man. This man's friends prayed to God for his health and God has heard their prayers."

"I have been sent by God to this man. God will heal this man through my hands."

Beathag came close to Manu. She spoke, "Ask for God's blessing and touch my hand."

Manu moved toward Beathag. He reached out his hand toward her and he spoke, "I ask the blessing of God that I may do the will of God."

Manu touched Beathag's hand. Beathag touched the leg of Manu.

Apophis gasped. Agymah gasped.

The leg of Manu changed color. The leg was not black. Manu's leg was as his other leg. Then, there was a sweet smell of flowers in the house. The smell of dead animals was gone.

Manu rose from his bed.

Agymah fell to his knees before Beathag. He spoke very quickly, "I ask the blessing of God that I may do the will of God."

Agymah touch the hand of Beathag and Beathag touch the hand of Agymah.

Beathag spoke, "The Holy Ghost came to me. God touched your hand through my hand. The power of God has healed you. You will follow the will of God."

Agymah spoke, "What do I do? How do I follow the will of God?"

Beathag spoke, "Follow your heart for God will lead you."

Agymah stood. He remembered the kettles of soup before the many houses. The servants prepared food from the scraps of his table. The soup was made from spoiled meat and vegetables.

Agymah spoke to Apophis, "Go to my house and prepare the best food and wine. When the food and wine are prepared, come to me. I will bring these people to my house that they may eat and drink."

Apophis spoke, "If the servants eat and drink, who will serve the servants?"

Agymah spoke, "These people have served me for many years. I will serve them."

Apophis left Agymah to order the food and wine prepared. Agymah looked at Beathag. He spoke saying, "I will witness God heal the child."

Beathag spoke, "No! When God heals the child, I will be alone with the child and the child's mother and father."

Agymah spoke, "I follow the will of God."

Beathag left the house of Manu and she walked to a small house, which was near. She entered the house to find a man, woman, and an infant boy.

The infant boy was ill with fever and the infant boy cried from fever.

Beathag spoke, "When I was an infant I was very sick. God sent a young boy to me. This boy had a gift from God. The gift from God was God healed through the hands of the young boy. The young boy touched me and God healed me through the young boy's hands."

"The gift God gave to the young boy God gave to me. God heals through my hands."

"It is time for God to pass the gift to another. God has sent me to your son. God will heal your son through my hands and God will heal no other through my hands. The gift God gave to me, God will give to your son. God will heal through the hands of your son."

Beathag spoke, "May I hold your son?"

רבקה

Dendera handed her son to Beathag. Beathag held him close and she whispered into his ear. The child's cries stopped.

Beathag spoke, "The power of God has healed your son."

Beathag passed her hand over the child. She looked upward and she whispered."

Beathag spoke, "It is the will of God that generations to come will know the power of God through the hands of a child. What was given to me has been taken from me. What was taken from me has been given to your son. God will heal through the hands of your son."

"Your son is protected by God himself. No man, woman, child, or beast of the earth shall harm your son. This is the will of God."

Beathag handed the child to Dendera and she spoke, "You are not of this place?"

Lateif, the father of Muslim, spoke, "We are from far away. Our place is east of the great river Nile. We have served Agymah for many years. Our place is far from here."

Beathag spoke, "Your son Muslim will serve God. Return to your place and share the blessing which God has given."

Lateif spoke, "We can not leave this place for Agymah will not allow us to leave. We are his servants. We are his property. Our son Muslim is his property."

Beathag spoke, "Agymah serves God. Agymah will allow you to leave for he follows the will of God."

And Lateif, Dendera, and Muslim went before Agymah. And Lateif told Agymah that God healed Musilm. Lateif told Agymah that it is the will of God that they return to their place east of the great river Nile.

And Agymah heard the words of Lateif. And Agymah, being of God, gave to them their freedom. And he gave to them food and coin. And Agymah sent many guards to take them to the river Nile.

And Lateif, Dendera, and Muslim left the place of Agymah to return to their place. And they were taken safely across the great river. And they traveled east from the great river to their place.

רבקה

רבקה
Tamiko

Near the base of the Altai Mountains, on the border of Mongolia and China, lies an unusual place. This unusual place is an area of ground barren of all things. There is no grass, trees, rocks, or soil within this area. This area forms a perfect circle six miles in diameter. Within this six mile circle is a smaller circle. The smaller circle is three hundred yards in diameter. The smaller circle is a perfect circle and within its boundaries lush grass and flowers grow.

When seen from the air, the two circles appear as a doughnut. Surrounding the large circle are many rocks, trees, plants, and grass.

The floor of the larger circle is perfectly level and smooth as glass. A builders level can be placed anywhere within the six mile circle and the level's bubble is perfectly centered.

The inner circle is three feet above the larger circle. The sides are smooth as glass.

The larger circle runs to the base of a small cliff. The side of the cliff, where the large circle stops, is smooth as glass.

No plants, grass, or trees will grow on the larger circle. Local residents attempted to build a wood and soil terrace within this area. Within several days, the wood and soil changed into a white powder. Then, the white powder slowly disappeared.

Many geologist and scientists have examined these two circles. In 1980, the two circles were measured using laser instruments. The two circles are perfect.

Geologists and scientists have attempted to explain this area. One suggestion is a meteor struck. However, no evidence of a meteor or an impact area can be found.

One suggestion is a comet exploded above the surface. However, there is no evidence of any explosion. The area is barren of all things. At the edge of the six-mile circle lush grass, trees, flowers, and plants grow.

One suggestion is the area is contaminated with radiation. There is no measurable radiation.

One suggestion is a native culture made the two circles. This suggestion has been discounted as no culture, past or present, could have made circles with perfect precision.

The circles are alleged to be many hundreds of years old. The exact date cannot be determined because there is nothing to carbon date.

The two circles and their origin is a mystery.

There is one additional suggestion as to how this area was formed. The suggestion is a local legend. The legend is many hundreds of years old.

The local residents call the area, Battle for the Sachi. Sachi is a Japanese word that means blessed.

Legend states that on this spot, ten thousand soldiers of the Imperial Guard battled the Father of All Things. The battle, which lasted but four crows of the cock, destroyed every soldier, horse, rock, tree, plant, blade of grass, and grain of soil within the six-mile radius.

Within the smaller circle, the Father of All Things protected twelve of the Imperial Guard, several wagons, several horses, and several people. One of the people was a young girl named Tamiko. Tamiko is a Japanese name that means, Child of the People.

According to this legend, the Father of All Things healed through the hands of Tamiko. Tamiko was taken to the emperor for the Father of All Things to heal his favorite wife.

The emperor's favorite wife was healed.

The child stayed at the palace of the emperor for many days. While at the palace, the Father of All Things healed many people through the hands of Tamiko.

A nephew of the emperor feared Tamiko had poisoned the emperor's mind for Tamiko spoke of the Father of All Things and his son. Tamiko told the emperor there were men coming to their country to tell stories of the son of the Father of All Things. These men would teach them of the son who died and returned from death. The son of the Father of All Things would save all mankind.

The child left the emperor's palace with a guard of twelve to journey to the west. The guard of twelve was to take Tamiko safely across the ocean and past the mountains to the far west.

The emperor's nephew sent his soldiers to murder the child. He ordered the soldiers to return with Tamiko's head upon a spear.

The soldiers followed the small group across the ocean to the base of the mountain. There, the soldiers waited to ambush the small group.

The soldiers hid behind the rocks and the soldiers hid in the trees. A large cavalry waited behind large rocks to charge the group from behind.

When the small group entered the road that lead through the mountain, the soldiers attacked from all sides.

When the soldiers attacked the small group, the Father of All Things surround the small group in a wall of white fire. No arrows or spears could pass the white fire. Many mounted soldiers charged the white fire only to become as of fire themselves.

The white fire grew larger and larger.

The soldiers battled from the rocks and the trees. The white fire burned through the rocks and burned through the trees to consume the soldiers. The soldiers on horse fled from the white fire only to be consumed as the white fire stretched outward in all directions.

The white fire grew faster than the horses of the soldiers could run.

The Battle for the Sachi lasted four crows of the cock.

In the end, the white fire consumed every soldier, horse, rock, tree, plant, blade of grass, and grain of soil. The small group was not harmed. The small group was protected within the circle of white fire.

The nephew of the emperor was executed for treason.

This story has been told for several hundred years and passed from generation to generation. The story begins by a small stream in Japan. The story ends at the base of the Altai Mountains on the border of Mongolia and China. The story ends at the place named, Battle for the Sachi. The story is titled, The Child of the People.

רבקה
The Child of the People

It was the custom in Japan to drown female children if the female child was the first birth. The female held a small worth in Japan. A male child could work in the fields. A female child may marry into a wealthy family. If there were little food, to feed the child would starve another child.

Unwanted children were either drowned or abandoned. The abandoned child would die from exposure of the weather.

Makoto and Machiko were very poor. They worked the land of another.

Machiko gave birth to a female. This was the first child of Machiko and Makoto. As was the custom, Machiko took the child to a stream to drown her.

However, Machiko loved her daughter and she could not bear to drown her. Machiko hid the child. She cared for her and the child grew in age.

Makoto became suspicious of Machiko. He had seen her leave their home and return many hours later. One day, Makoto followed her. He followed her to a small house in a wooded area.

Makoto found Machiko with their infant daughter. The child was near one year of birth and the child was ill was fever. Makoto was angry with Machiko. He ordered she drown the girl.

Machiko took her daughter, who was unnamed, to the stream to drown her. She took a small silk bag. She would place stones in the bag, with her daughter, and throw the bag into the stream.

Machiko's heart was heavy, as she loved her daughter. Machiko believed Makoto also loved his daughter. She knew that he had knowledge of the child but she was ordered to drown their daughter.

As she walked to the stream, she passed an old woman. The old woman was sitting at the side of the road. The old woman was blind.

As she neared the old woman, the old woman spoke, "You will not succeed. The child you carry will return this way."

Machiko was startled by her words. The old woman looked at Machiko. Her eyes were as the eyes of the dead. The old woman's eyes were black.

Machiko asked, "What do you speak? Here is a coin."

The old woman responded, "I speak of truth. I do not want a coin."

Machiko responded, "If you do not want a coin, what do you want?"

The old woman replied, "I only ask to confess my misgivings and ask forgiveness from the one who is all. I ask to touch the child."

Machiko was upset by her words. She hurried toward the stream.

Machiko came to the stream and she kneeled with her daughter. Her daughter was very sick and she was crying. Machiko wanted to help her but soon she would not be sick.

Machiko took the silk bag and she placed several stones in the bottom of the bag. She was to place her daughter in the bag when she heard a voice.

She turned to see a young boy. The boy was but eight summers in age. The boy spoke, "You will not succeed for the Father of All Things does not will it so."

Machiko was startled. She asked, "Who are you?"

The boy spoke, "My name is Kado. I have been sent by the Father of All Things to heal your daughter. I have been sent by the Father of All Things to heal your heart."

Machiko asked, "Who is this person you speak of?"

The boy spoke, "The Father of All Things is the creator of all."

Machiko asked, "How will you heal my daughter?"

Kado spoke, "When I was an infant I was very sick. A young girl came to me. This girl had a gift. The Father of All Things healed through her hands. The young girl touched me and the Father of All Things healed me. The gift of the young girl was taken from her and given to me. The Father of All Things heals through my hands."

"The Father of All Things will heal your daughter through my hands. May I hold your daughter?"

Machiko was upset by what this young boy spoke. She was unsure but her daughter was very ill. She handed her daughter to him.

The young boy held Machiko's daughter. He held her close and he whispered into her ear. The child stopped crying.

The young boy spoke, "The power of the Father of All Things has healed your daughter."

The young boy then passed his hand over the young girl. He looked upward and whispered.

The young boy spoke, "It is the will of the Father of All Things that generations to come will know his power through the hands of a child. What was given to me has been taken from me. What was taken from me has been given to your daughter. The Father of All Things will heal through your daughter's hands."

"Your daughter is protected by the Father of All Things himself. No man, woman, child, or beast of the earth shall harm your daughter. This is his will."

The young boy spoke again, "You have not named your daughter. Her name shall be Tamiko, Child of the People."

"Return to your place and share the blessing which the Father of All Things has given."

The young boy returned Tamiko to Machiko. He then turned and he walked away.

Machiko was upset by these events. She looked at her daughter. Her daughter looked well. The fever was gone.

She thought about these events. She had been ordered by her husband to drown their daughter.

Machiko placed her daughter in the silk bag. She tied the top and she threw the bag into the stream.

The bag made a splash when it struck the water. Machiko watched for the bag to sink but the bag did not sink. She waited for the bag to sink but the bag did not sink.

Machiko was upset. She thought, 'There is not enough weight of stone.'

Machiko went into the water to retrieve the bag. When she picked up the bag, the bag was not wet. There was no water on the bag.

Machiko opened the bag. Her daughter smiled. There was no water on her clothes. Machiko placed more stone in the bag. She tied the top and she threw the bag into the stream.

The bag did not sink.

Machiko again retrieved the bag. The bag was not wet. Machiko opened the bag. Her daughter smiled. There was no water on her clothes.

Machiko again placed more stone in the bag. The bag was very heavy with the stone. She walked into the water and she released the bag.

The bag did not sink.

Machiko remembered the words of the young boy, 'You will not succeed for the Father of All Things does not will it so."

'Your daughter is protected by the Father of All Things himself. No man, woman, child, or beast of the earth shall harm your daughter. This is his will."

Machiko remembered his other words, 'I have been sent by the Father of All Things to heal your daughter. I have been sent by the Father of All Things to heal your heart."

Machiko could not drown her daughter. She loved her daughter. Machiko quickly reached for the bag. She untied the top and she pulled her daughter from the bag. When Machiko pulled her daughter from the bag, the bag sank into the water.

Machiko hugged her daughter and she repeated the name, "Tamiko." She hurried home.

As she walked on the road, she came to the old blind woman.

As she neared the old woman, the old woman spoke, "You did not succeed. The child you carried has returned this way. The child you carry is not the one before."

Machiko stopped. She looked at the old woman and she asked, "Of what do you speak?"

The old woman responded, "I speak of truth. I only ask to confess my misgivings and ask forgiveness from the one who is all. I ask to touch the child."

Machiko asked, "Why do you wish to touch my child?"

The old woman replied, "I dreamed of a child who is Sachi. I was told to come to this road and wait for the child. I am to confess my misgivings and ask forgiveness of the one who is all. If I touch the child and the child touches me, the one who is all will give me sight."

Machiko was confused. She asked, "Why would the one who is all return the sight of an old woman? You have few days."

The old woman replied, "The one who is all will not return my sight for me. He will return my sight for you."

Machiko asked, "Of what use is your sight for me? I can not see through your eyes."

The old woman replied, "The one is who is all will open my eyes. The one who is all will open your eyes."

Machiko asked, "What will I see?"

The old woman replied, "Truth."

Machiko asked, "And what is truth?"

The old woman replied, "Truth is the words of the young boy at the stream. All he said is truth. When my eyes are opened, your eyes will open."

The old woman spoke again, "I have done many things which were against others. I ask forgiveness for all which I have done."

The old woman stood and she walked toward Machiko. She held out her hand and she touched Tamiko.

When the old woman touched Tamiko, Tamiko touched her arm.

The old woman bent her head downward. She looked up and she opened her eyes.

Machiko gasped. The old woman's eyes were no longer the eyes of the dead. Her eyes were opened and she could see.

The old woman spoke, "The one who is all has healed me through the hands of the child. Your eyes have been opened as my eyes have been opened. You will see truth."

The old woman picked up a small bag and she walked away from Machiko.

Machiko could not believe what had happened. Truly, the young boy spoke truth. The bag did not sink. The old woman's sight was returned when she touched Tamiko and Tamiko touched her. Truly, Tamiko was Sachi.

Machiko hurried home. When she neared her home, Makoto was waiting for her.

Makoto ran to Machiko. "You did not drown our daughter! I am happy!" he said.

Makoto added, "I feel asleep and I dreamed of days to come. In my dream, the Father of All Things spoke to me. He told me he would heal many people through the hands of our daughter. He told me her name is to be Tamiko - Child of the People."

"Is it true?"

Machiko spoke, "Yes! It is true! We met an old woman who is blind. The old woman asked forgiveness. She touched Tamiko and Tamiko touched her. The Father of All Things returned the woman's sight."

Makoto spoke, "I believe you. It is true."

Machiko and Makoto stayed at their home for many days. During those days, many people came to their home to see the Sachi. There were many people who were sick that came to their home. The people asked for forgiveness from the Father of All Things.

They touched Tamiko and Tamiko touched them. The Father of All Things healed everyone who touched Tamiko and were touched by her.

Then one night, Makoto had a dream. In this dream he was told to take his wife and their child to a far place.

Six Years Later

The young boy came running into the tent. He yelled, "Soldiers! Soldiers!"

There were several people in the tent. The elder of the village, Kazuo, stood up and he went to the tent opening. He looked out.

As far as he could see there were soldiers. Two soldiers road side by side. Each soldier carried the imperial banner. The soldiers were the Imperial Guard of the emperor. He looked closely; the soldiers did not bear arms.

The column stopped near the village and four soldiers dismounted. The four soldiers walked toward his tent.

Kazuo walked toward the four soldiers.

The four soldiers bowed before him.

Kazuo returned the bow.

One of the soldiers spoke, "I bring greetings from the emperor. We travel in search of a child. The child is Sachi. Do you have knowledge of the child?"

Kazuo spoke, "Yes. The child is here."

The soldier became very excited. He spoke very quickly to the soldier beside him. The soldier ran to the column of soldiers.

The soldier ordered four to return to the emperor. When the soldier said they had found the Sachi, the soldiers cheered. Then, many soldiers rode from the column.

Kazuo asked, "What do you want of the Sachi?"

The soldier spoke, "The emperor's favorite wife is ill. The emperor was told of the Sachi. We have been ordered to find the Sachi and take her to the emperor."

Makoto was in the tent of Kazuo. He heard these words and he came from the tent.

Makoto asked, "If we refuse will you take us by force?"

The soldier looked at Makoto. He bowed to Makoto and he spoke, "I misspoke. We have been ordered to find the Sachi."

Makoto asked, "If we refuse to come what will happen to us?"

The soldier spoke, "I am to persuade you to come of your own will. The emperor will give you anything you ask. I have been given the power to grant your request."

Makoto spoke, "The Sachi is named Tamiko. She is my daughter. What does the emperor know of her?"

The soldier spoke, "The emperor knows of the Sachi. She has the power to heal the sick."

Makoto spoke, "The emperor has not been told correctly. Tamiko has no power. The Father of All Things heals through her hands. The Father of All Things has the power."

The soldier asked, "Is it not true that the child can touch a person and that person will be healed?"

Makoto spoke, "Yes. That is true. It is the Father of All Things who heals."

The soldier asked, "Will you come with us to the emperor's wife? The emperor will grant any request you make."

Makoto spoke, "These people have little food. Their crops did not yield much grain. Will the emperor give to them food to last the winter? Will the emperor help these people?"

The soldier replied, "If that is your request, I have been given power to grant it."

Makoto spoke, "We travel to the west across the ocean. I have been told of many bandits. Will the emperor give us safe passage to the mountains west of the ocean?"

The soldier replied, "If that is your request, I have been given power to grant it."

Makoto spoke, "We will come with you."

The soldier replied, "What other requests do you have?"

Makoto spoke, "None. If the emperor will help these people and give us safe passage, we have no other request."

The soldier asked, "Do you not request money? Do you not request land? The emperor will give to you all these things."

Makoto spoke, "We ask nothing for ourselves."

The soldier bowed to Makoto. He slowly rose and smiled. He spoke, "Your requests will be granted."

The soldier spoke to the soldier next to him. He said, "Send runners to the emperor. We are bringing the Sachi. Tell the emperor of the requests."

The soldier ran to the column of soldiers. He spoke very quickly. Four soldiers broke rank and they began riding to the rear of the column.

Makoto asked, "When do we leave?"

"Now!" the soldier replied.

Makoto looked to see a small wagon coming toward them. There were six horses pulling the wagon. The wagon was very small and light in weight. The horses were very large and powerful.

Makoto spoke, "We will get what is ours."

The soldier spoke, "There is no time. We have all you will need."

The soldier yelled to the column to dismount and bring their food. The soldiers dismounted and opened their food bags. A soldier pulled a small wagon near the soldiers. As he passed each soldier, the soldier placed his food bag in the wagon.

Makoto asked, "What are they doing?"

The soldier replied, "It will be many days before food can be brought to this village. We will give these people the food we have."

Makoto asked, "What will the soldiers eat?"

The soldier replied, "We are the Imperial Guard. We are the strongest and the bravest. Each soldier is loyal to the emperor. They can go many days without food or water. They freely give their food for the emperor and the Sachi."

Makoto watched the soldier walk to his horse. The soldier opened his food bag. The soldier placed his food bag in the wagon.

Several soldiers unloaded the collected food from the wagon. Makoto looked at the food. There was enough food to last many days, perhaps many weeks.

When the food was unloaded, the soldier asked, "Where is the Sachi?"

"She is here," Makoto said.

As Makoto spoke, His wife Machiko and their daughter Tamiko came from the tent of Kazuo.

The soldier looked at Tamiko. Tamiko was but seven summers of age. She was very small and light in body. Tamiko's hair was long and braided.

The soldier bowed to Tamiko.

Tamiko returned the bow.

"We must hurry! Death waits at the door," the soldier said.

The small wagon was ready for them to enter. Makoto looked at the horses. It was many days to the emperor. These horses were strong and the wagon was light in weight. These horses would take many days to reach the city.

They entered the wagon to find many soft covers of silk. There were silken braids for handles and there were two women to serve them. The two women bowed to them.

The soldier spoke, "We will travel with the speed of the hawk. Forgive me if the journey is not pleasant."

The driver raised the imperial flag on the wagon. The imperial flag was a signal that the emperor or his immediate family was in the wagon.

When the imperial flag was raised, each soldier kneeled and bowed toward the wagon.

The wagon began to move slowly. Then, the horses began to move faster. As the wagon passed the soldiers, each soldier stood and cheered.

The wagon began to move faster and faster. The driver whipped the horses into a fast run. The speed was faster than any Makoto had seen. Faster and faster the horses ran.

"These horses can not run at this speed for days," Makoto said.

Faster and faster the horses ran. The wagon was light in weight and the horses were large and strong. Such speed he had never seen.

There were many soldiers riding beside the wagon and their horses could not run with the wagon. Slowly, the horses of the soldiers fell behind.

Faster and faster the horses ran as the driver cracked his whip.

Makoto spoke, "We travel with the speed of the hawk."

Makoto felt the wagon begin to slow. 'The horses are tired,' he thought. Makoto looked out of the wagon.

The horses were not tired. There before them was a large group of soldiers. Waiting for them was another wagon. The wagon was as the one they rode. There were six fresh horses and a different driver.

As they approached, the soldiers kneeled and bowed to the wagon.

The wagon stopped and the soldier said, "Quickly! We must change wagons. Death waits at the door."

They quickly left the wagon. When they left the wagon, the imperial flag was lowered. When they entered the new wagon, the imperial flag was raised on the new wagon.

The wagon was as the one before. There were two women to serve them. Within the wagon were food, drink, and fresh clothes.

The soldier spoke, "We will travel with the speed of the hawk. Forgive me if the journey is not pleasant."

The wagon began to move slowly. Then, the horses began to move faster. As the wagon passed the soldiers, each soldier stood and cheered.

Faster and faster the horses ran. "Such speed," Makoto said.

They traveled from wagon to wagon. When it seemed the horses were tired, there was a new wagon waiting for them. Each wagon they rode flew the imperial flag.

For two days they traveled with the speed of the hawk.

On the morning of the third day the wagon began to slow.

Makoto looked out of the wagon. He saw many soldiers but there was no new wagon. As they approached the soldiers, the soldiers kneeled and bowed to the imperial flag.

Makoto asked, "What is wrong?"

The soldier replied, "Nothing is wrong. We wait."

"Why do we wait?" Makoto asked.

The soldier pointed ahead.

Makoto looked ahead to see a large cloud of dust. He looked closer and he could see many soldiers and wagons. The wagons were heavy and oxen pulled them.

"What is this?" Makoto asked.

The soldier replied, "This is your first request."

The column of soldiers and wagons stopped.

"We move on," the soldier said.

Their wagon began to move slowly toward the column of soldiers and wagons.

Makoto looked at the column of soldiers and wagons. He saw the soldiers dismount. He saw many people leave the wagons. The soldiers and the people stood beside the wagons. As their wagon approached, the soldiers and the people kneeled and bowed before the imperial flag.

Their wagon moved slowly past the column of wagons. Makoto began to count the wagons. He counted ten, twenty, thirty, maybe a hundred wagons. Each wagon was filled. Beside the wagons, soldiers, men, women, and children kneeled and bowed.

"What is this?" Makoto asked.

"The soldier replied, "This is your first request. You asked the emperor to help the people of the village."

Makoto said, "I asked for food to last through the winter. Your soldiers have given much food. This is not food?"

The soldier replied, "The emperor was pleased with your request. You could have had anything you wished. The emperor would give you money, land, and power. You asked nothing for yourself. You asked for others."

"The emperor granted your request. The emperor increased your request one thousand times. The wagons are filled with food, medicine, wood, cloth, and seed. Before you are healers, teachers, and craftsmen. The emperor has sent craftsmen to teach the villagers their skill. The teachers will teach the villagers to read and write. The villagers will be taught how to plant and harvest the seed. There are animals for food. There are horses and wagons."

"What you see is one of six. The emperor will build a city where the village lies."

Makoto spoke, "This is more than I asked. I asked only for food for the winter."

The soldier smiled. He asked, "Are you not pleased?"

Makoto shook his head. "Yes, I am pleased," he said.

Their wagon had passed the many wagons. The driver whipped the horses into a fast run. As their wagon passed the last wagon, the soldiers, men, women, and children stood and cheered.

The wagon continued on. Makoto tried to calculate the distance they had traveled. He believed the village was seven suns from the imperial palace. They had traveled for three suns. He could see the mountains that lay south of the imperial palace. They had traveled seven suns in three. They were close to the imperial palace.

The wagon began to slow. Makoto looked out of the wagon. Such a sight he had not seen.

Before him were many soldiers. There, with the soldiers, was a wagon he had never seen. The wagon was as the one they rode. Before the wagon were twelve horses.

Their wagon slowed and a soldier rode to their wagon. He spoke quickly to the soldier and he rode off. Many soldiers followed him.

The soldier spoke, "Quickly! Death waits at the door. This wagon is too slow. The craftsmen prepared a special wagon. This wagon will take us to the palace."

"The emperor has placed his favorite wife outside the palace."

They quickly changed wagons. This wagon was as the one before. There was food, drink, and two women to serve them.

The driver raised the imperial flag and the soldiers kneeled and bowed. The wagon started very slow. Then the wagon began to go faster. When the wagon passed the soldiers, the soldiers cheered.

The soldiers chanted, "Sachi! Sachi! Sachi!"

This wagon was faster than any other. Truly, they traveled with the speed of the hawk.

As they neared the palace, Makoto could see a large tent outside the palace. The imperial flag flew over the tent.

Their wagon rode quickly toward the tent. The wagon stopped outside the tent and they were taken quickly inside.

The tent was spectacular. There were silks and food. Many guards stood at attention. There were many people within the tent. Near the center of the tent was a large bed.

The favorite wife of the emperor was lying on the bed. She was very ill with fever. The emperor himself came to them.

The emperor spoke, "My wife is ill. I ask the Father of All Things to heal my wife."

The emperor bowed before Tamiko.

Tamiko returned his bow.

When the emperor bowed, everyone present gasped. Never had the emperor bowed to anyone.

The emperor spoke, "I bow not to the Sachi. I bow to the Father of All Things."

The emperor bowed again.

Tamiko returned his bow.

The people present gasped.

Tamiko went to the bed of the emperor's favorite wife. She kneeled before the bed.

Tamiko asked, "Do you ask forgiveness of the Father of All Things?

The emperor's wife spoke, "I have done many things of which I am ashamed. I ask forgiveness for those things."

The emperor's favorite wife reached out to Tamiko. She held Tamiko's hand and Tamiko touched her hand.

The emperor's wife rose from her bed.

The people present gasped for the emperor's wife had been healed of her sickness.

The emperor was overjoyed. He proclaimed a day of rest and feast. The many people began to talk amongst themselves.

Tamiko, Makoto, and Machiko were taken to the palace to rest and bathe.

Many days passed and Tamiko was summoned before the emperor and his favorite wife. They asked many questions of her.

Tamiko spoke to the emperor of the Father of All Things and his son. Such words the emperor had not heard.

Many people came to the palace to see Tamiko. Many people were sick. These people asked to see Tamiko. The emperor allowed the people in. The emperor witnessed many people healed. He witnessed the wealthy and powerful healed. He witnessed the poor and outcast healed. The Father of All Things healed all who asked for forgiveness.

Makoto, Machiko, and Tamiko stayed at the palace for many days. Soon, they would leave.

One morning, Makoto walked near the gates of the palace. There, he saw many wagons. Twelve soldiers stood guard over the wagons. As he approached the wagons, the soldier who escorted him from the village approached him.

The soldier bowed to Makoto.

Makoto returned the bow. He looked at the soldier. "I do not know your name," he said.

The soldier spoke, "My name is Shiro. I am the fourth born of Kentaro. I am a general to the emperor. "

Makoto bowed to Shiro.

Makoto pointed to the wagons. He asked, "Is the emperor leaving the city?"

Shiro spoke, "This is your second request."

Makoto said, "My second request was safe passage across the ocean to the mountains to the west. There are many wagons."

Shiro spoke, "The emperor was pleased with your request. He has increased your request one thousand times."

"These wagons will take you to the ocean. There are ships waiting to take you safely across the ocean and these wagons will be taken apart and loaded onto the ships. When you have crossed the ocean, these wagons will be put together. These wagons will take you to your destination."

Makoto spoke, "I only asked for safe passage across the ocean to the mountains. We will travel west past the mountains. I do not know our final destination."

Shiro spoke, "The emperor orders these men to guard and protect you to your destination. When you have reached your destination, they will return."

Makoto spoke, "I have heard of many bandits. There are only twelve guards?"

Shiro spoke, "These twelve men are samurai. The emperor personally chose these men. These men are the best of the Imperial Guard. Each man is skilled in battle and each man can defeat one hundred in battle."

"These men are loyal to the emperor. These men are loyal to the Sachi."

Makoto asked, "When will we leave?"

Shiro spoke, "They will leave at your orders. They wait for your order to leave."

Makoto spoke, "We leave tomorrow morning."

The following morning, Makoto, Machiko, and Tamiko appeared before the emperor. The emperor spoke, "The Father of All Things has healed my favorite wife and many others. I bid you farewell. It is my command that your journey will be pleasant."

Makoto bowed and he spoke to the emperor, "The Father of All Things guides Tamiko. It is his will we journey west past the ocean and the mountains. We do not know where he will lead us. We travel to do his will."

The emperor spoke, "The Sachi spoke many things of the Father of All Things and his son. Of these things, we have no knowledge. We await others who will bring us knowledge of the son of the Father of All Things."

The emperor bowed before Tamiko.

The people present gasped. Again, the emperor bowed before another.

The emperor spoke, "I bow before the Father of All Things. It was his power that healed my favorite wife. It was his will which brought the Sachi before us. It was his will that we be made known of his son. It is his will which takes the Sachi from us to others."

Makoto, Machiko, and Tamiko bowed to the emperor.

They left the palace to the wagons that waited for them. When they entered the wagons, the wagons were filled with food, drink, and clothing. Two women were there to serve them.

Makoto looked for Shiro. He had searched for him in the palace but he did not see him. Makoto asked of Shiro. No one knew where he was. Makoto wanted to speak to Shiro before he left. Shiro was not present.

They were taken to the ocean where two ships waited. Many soldiers quickly dismantled the wagons and loaded them onto the ships. The ships sailed across the ocean to the mainland of Cathay. There, the soldiers reassembled the wagons.

They began their long journey west past the mountains.

It was at this time, the nephew of the emperor was gathering soldiers. The emperor's nephew was angered at the words spoken of the Father of All Things. The Father of All Things treated everyone equal. This was not to be.

Shiro was with the emperor's nephew. The emperor's nephew wanted Shiro to gather soldiers for him. The emperor's nephew wanted to murder the Sachi. The emperor's nephew wanted to prove that the Father of All Things was a myth. He would bring the head of the Sachi to the emperor.

Shiro would not agree. Shiro stated that it was the emperor's command that the Sachi be given safe passage to her destination. Shiro would not violate the emperor's command.

Shiro and the emperor's nephew argued. Shiro would not agree to gather soldiers to murder the Sachi.

The emperor's nephew wanted to murder Shiro but it was forbidden. Shiro was a general to the emperor. Only the emperor could order the death of Shiro.

A soldier of the emperor, named Tanaka, came to the emperor's nephew. He agreed to gather soldiers loyal to the emperor's nephew. He gathered ten thousand soldiers.

Tanaka gathered the soldiers in secret. He obtained a copy of the map that had been given to the samurai who guarded the Sachi. The map was marked where the samurai would take the Sachi. Tanaka would take his soldiers to the base of the mountain and ambush them. There, they would murder the Sachi and bring her head to the emperor's nephew. The Sachi's head would be placed before the gates of the palace that all might see.

The emperor's nephew ordered Tanaka to build a shrine where they murdered the Sachi. The shrine would forever mark the place where the Sachi died. The shrine would be a sign to the world that the Father of All Things is a myth.

Secretly, Tanaka gathered the soldiers. In secret, they traveled to the ocean. There, they took ships across the ocean to the mainland of Cathay. The Sachi was many weeks ahead of them. Tanaka led the soldiers west to the base of the mountain.

Tanaka and his soldiers had been gone for many days when Shiro learned of the plot to murder the Sachi. Shiro went to the emperor and he spoke of the nephew's plan.

The emperor immediately ordered Shiro to pursue Tanaka. Shiro was to prevent Tanaka and his soldiers from murdering the Sachi.

Shiro quickly gathered soldiers. Word quickly spread of the plot to murder the Sachi. Many soldiers came to Shiro. These soldiers pledged their swords and their lives to defend the Sachi. The Sachi was under the protection of the emperor.

The soldiers loyal to the emperor numbered forty thousand.

Quickly, Shiro and the forty thousand soldiers pursued Tanaka and his ten thousand soldiers.

The soldiers marched to the ocean. There, many ships took them across the ocean to the mainland of Cathay. They marched west to the mountains.

Many weeks passed and there was no word of the Sachi, Tanaka, or Shiro. The emperor was very worried that his soldiers had fought one another. Such a battle would divide his country. There were warrior clans gathering to battle for control.

The emperor was worried that the Sachi had been murdered.

Many more weeks passed and there was no word of the Sachi, Tanaka, or Shiro.

The weeks turned into months.

Then, one morning, a soldier rode into the city. The soldier spoke that Shiro and the forty thousand soldiers were at the ocean. Shiro was coming with news of the battle.

When Shiro arrived at the palace, he was quickly taken before the emperor. The room was filled with many people as they waited for news of Tanaka and the Sachi.

Shiro came before the emperor. He bowed.

The emperor asked, "Is the Sachi dead?"

Shiro responded, "No."

The people gasped.

The emperor asked, "Did you battle Tanaka?"

Shiro responded, "No."

The people gasped.

The emperor asked, "Where is Tanaka?"

Shiro responded, "I do not know."

The people gasped.

The emperor spoke, "I do not wish to hear riddles. Where is Tanaka?"

Shiro responded, "I do not know."

The people gasped.

The emperor asked, "If Tanaka did not murder the Sachi what happened to Tanaka?"

Shiro responded, "We were told the Father of All Thing destroyed Tanaka and his soldiers in a wall of white fire."

The people gasped.

The emperor asked, "What happened to the Sachi?"

Shiro spoke, "We followed Tanaka and his soldiers to the base of the great mountain west of the ocean."

"When we came to the base of the mountain, there was a place barren of all things. There are no trees, rocks, plants, grass, or soil. There is nothing."

The people gasped.

Shiro continued, "Within this area barren of all things is an area where lush grass and flowers grow. Within this area are the tracks of many wagons and horses. These tracks point toward the road which leads into the mountains."

The people gasped.

Shiro continued, "This area barren of all things is larger than the palace. The ground is as polished jade. Many horses fell for they could not walk on the ground. The soldiers dismounted for their horses could not stand on the ground. The soldiers pushed the wagons for the horses could not pull the wagons. The wheels of the wagons turned without moving the wagons."

The people gasped.

Shiro continued, "There was nothing here. Nothing. We looked for Tanaka and his soldiers. We found nothing. We looked for the Sachi. We found nothing."

The people gasped.

Shiro continued, "We camped near this place which is barren of all things. I sent many soldiers into the mountains. I sent one soldier to follow the road which lead into the mountain."

"The many soldiers returned after many days. They found nothing.

"The one soldier returned after many days. He found many wagon and horse tracks on the road. The tracks were far into the mountains."

"We quickly broke camp and we followed the tracks into the mountains. We traveled for many days and we came to a village. It was here we learned of the fate of Tanaka and his ten thousand soldiers."

"The Father of All Things destroyed Tanaka and his ten thousand soldiers in a wall of white fire."

The people gasped.

The emperor asked, "What of the Sachi? Where is she?"

Shiro spoke, "The Sachi is alive and well. It was the tracks of the wagons of the Sachi and the tracks of the horses of the twelve samurai we followed into the mountain. The people in the village have seen the Sachi. It was Makoto and the twelve samurai who told the villagers of the fate of Tanaka."

The emperor asked, "What happened to Tanaka?"

Shiro spoke, "Makoto and the twelve samurai told the villagers that Tanaka and his soldiers ambushed them at the base of the mountain. The twelve samurai did not know of the ambush. They were surprised when the soldiers of the emperor attacked them. Tanaka himself led the attack."

"Tanaka's soldiers were in the rocks and the trees. A large cavalry attacked from behind. Tanaka's soldiers attacked from all sides."

"When Tanaka's soldiers attacked, the Father of All Things placed a wall of white fire around their wagons and horses."

"The wall of white fire was as fine silk and the wall of white fire was higher than the walls of the palace. They could see through the fire."

The people gasped.

Shiro continued, "The archers released many arrows. When the arrows touched the wall of white fire, the arrows became as of fire."

The people gasped.

Shiro continued, "The soldiers released many arrows and the soldiers threw many spears. No arrow or spear passed the white fire. Many soldiers charged the white fire only to become as of fire themselves."

The people gasped.

Shiro continued, "Then, it happened."

The emperor asked, "What happened?"

Shiro continued, "The white fire began to grow."

The people gasped.

Shiro continued, "The white fire grew larger and larger. The soldiers on horse turned their horses from the white fire. They ran from the white fire. The white fire grew faster than the horses could run. The white fire consumed the soldiers and their horses."

The people gasped.

Shiro continued, "The white fire grew in all directions. Everything the white fire touched became as fire and burned away. The white fire burned everything."

"Soldiers battled from behind rocks and soldiers battled in the trees. The white fire burned through the rocks and burned through the trees to consume the soldiers."

The people gasped.

Shiro continued, "The battle lasted but four crows of the cock. When the battle was over every soldier, horse, rock, tree, plant, blade of grass, and grain of soil was consumed."

The people gasped.

Shiro continued, "The Sachi, twelve samurai, their wagons, and their horses were not harmed. They were protected within the circle of white fire."

The emperor asked, "Do you know this is truth?"

Shiro spoke, "We do not know this is truth. We followed the tracks of Tanaka and his men to this place barren of all things. The tracks end at the edge of this place. The tracks go in. The tracks do not come out."

"The only tracks which left this area were the tracks of the Sachi's wagons and the tracks of the horses of the twelve samurai."

"We do know the Sachi passed this area. Many villagers in the mountains have seen her."

"We do know that Tanaka and his men did not enter the mountains for no villager has seen Tanaka or his men."

"We do know that Tanaka and his men can not be found. And we know of this place."

"Many soldiers have seen this place. Such a place we have not seen. The villagers named this place, Battle for the Sachi."

The emperor called his nephew before him.

The emperor spoke, "If the Father of All Things destroyed the soldiers of Tanaka with his fire, the Father of All Things can give or take life as his will. The Father of All Things can build or destroy cities."

"It was your will to murder the Sachi and place a shrine to your victory where she died. There is a shrine. The shrine is to the Father of All Things."

"My fear is the Father of All Things will turn his head from us."

"You sought to murder the Sachi and place her head upon a spear that all may see. The fate you planned for the Sachi will be your fate."

The nephew of the emperor was taken away and he was executed for treason. His head was placed upon a spear and the spear was placed by the palace gates for all to see.

רבקה

Timothy

The soldier entered the tent. Graham was standing near a table made of wood placed on stone. On the table was a map. Graham was looking at the map. When the soldier entered the tent Graham looked up and he asked, "Any change?"

The soldier answered, "None. The boy spoke to me."

Graham looked up quickly, "What did he say?"

The soldier answered, "The same as yesterday but today he said something else."

Graham moved toward the soldier, "What did he say?"

The soldier spoke, "He said the same thing as yesterday and the day before. He said it was God's will that he leave. He said we are to release the others."

Graham spoke, "This I know. What else did he say?"

The soldier spoke, "The boy Timothy said we have two days to release him and the others."

Graham asked, "Two days? What will happen in two days?"

The soldier spoke, "The boy Timothy said if he and the others are not released, God will send his angel to deliver them. The angel of God will come the morning of the third day."

Graham spoke, "Quickly! I must go to Timothy."

They hurried from the tent. Outside the tent were many tents. Among the tents was a stockade. Within the stockade were several men. The men were monks.

Graham went to the stockade gate. He spoke, "We mean you no harm. We await word from Elizabeth."

One of the monks came to the stockade gate. He spoke, "God sends Timothy to Scotland to do his will."

The monk added, "Release Timothy! Release us!"

Graham responded, "Timothy is not being held. Only you are being held."

The monk responded, "Timothy will not leave without us. Timothy follows the will of God. We follow the will of God."

Graham spoke, "A few days more. We ask a few days more."

The monk spoke, "God does not wait for kings or queens."

The monk turned away from Graham. He walked away from the stockade gate toward the other monks. He sat on the ground beside them.

Graham walked quickly to a tent near the stockade.

Outside the tent were two guards. When Graham approached the tent, the guards allowed Graham to enter. There were three people inside the tent. The boy, Timothy, was but eight years of age. Timothy sat on the ground. His father and his mother sat beside him.

Graham spoke to Timothy, "Are you comfortable?"

Timothy did not answer.

Graham spoke again, "A few days. All I ask is a few more days. I am sure Elizabeth will come."

Timothy looked upward to Graham. He spoke, "The angel of God will deliver us in two days."

Graham kneeled before Timothy, "We mean you no harm. We have not harmed you."

"You must understand. If Elizabeth sees you, if she knows of you, the religious battle will be over."

Timothy spoke, "I follow the will of God. It is God's will I leave England and journey to Scotland."

Graham spoke, "You must understand Elizabeth must see you. She must speak to you."

Timothy spoke, "In two days the angel of God will deliver us."

Graham stood quickly. He turned and he left the tent.

Graham hurried back to his tent. The soldier was waiting for him in the tent. When Graham entered the tent the soldier spoke, "We lost more men."

Graham asked, "How many?"

The soldier replied, "Fifty, maybe one hundred. They are afraid."

Graham asked, "How many are left?"

The soldier responded, "One thousand today. I do not know how many tomorrow."

Graham walked to the table and he looked at the map. The map was a drawing of the border of England and Scotland. He looked at the soldier. "Has Mary abdicated?" he asked.

The soldier responded, "I do not know. We have heard nothing."

Graham asked, "Any sign of the Scots?"

The soldier responded, "No."

Graham spoke, "Mary does not know."

The soldier responded, "I think not. If she knew there would be many Scots at the border."

The soldier asked, "Are you going to release them?"

Graham responded, "I can't."

The soldier asked, "Do you believe what the boy said? The boy said God will send his angel to deliver them."

Graham moved from the table. He folded his arms across his chest and he paced before the table. He quickly sat down and he placed his hands over his face. "I do not know what to believe," he said.

The soldier spoke, "It happened again today."

Graham asked, "Who was it this time?"

The soldier spoke, "It was an old woman. She was very sick. Several men carried her into the boy's tent. The old woman was carried into the tent and she walked out."

"The soldiers saw this. They are afraid of what you do."

"What will you do?"

Graham spoke, "Wait. We wait for Elizabeth."

One day passed and Graham had not received word from Elizabeth. He had sent word to Elizabeth of a child healed by God and blessed by God. God healed through the hands of the child. He had seen this with his own eyes. It was true.

Graham wanted Elizabeth to see the child. He wanted her to talk to the child. Mary of Guise abolished the Roman Catholic Church in Scotland. Mary was rumored to abdicate in favor of her son James. England was becoming Protestant.

He hoped Elizabeth could convince the child to come to London. Perhaps they could learn of the true church from the child. Perhaps they could put this religious war to sleep.

Graham walked to the front of his tent. He thought to himself, 'Did I do wrong?'

Graham had heard of the child and he was told the child was leaving England to journey to Scotland. He quickly gathered his army and they stopped the young boy before he could cross the English border.

The boy traveled with his father, mother, and several monks. His soldiers were afraid of the boy. They would not touch him for he was of God. He could not stop the boy but he could stop the monks.

The monks were placed in a stockade and they were kept from crossing the English border. The boy would not leave them.

Tomorrow, the angel of God would come.

The soldier came to Graham's tent. "He wants to see you," he said.

Graham quickly went to the boy's tent.

Graham walked into the tent. "You asked to see me?"

Timothy spoke, "Tomorrow the sun will rise and the angel of God will come to deliver us. If you do not release us, the angel of God will destroy you and all who stand with you."

Graham spoke, "We have a thousand men."

Timothy replied, "The angel of God will defeat one thousand times one thousand."

Graham spoke, "You must understand. We mean you no harm. I want you to speak to Elizabeth. We want to know of which church God commands we follow."

Timothy replied, "All you wish to know has been spoken. All you wish to know will be written."

Graham pleaded with Timothy, "A few days. Give us a few days."

Timothy replied, "God waits for no man. Tomorrow, the angel of God comes to deliver us. Look for him in the east."

Graham quickly left.

Late in the day, Graham stood by his tent and he watched the sun set. There was no word from Elizabeth.

Graham could not sleep. He paced the inside of his tent waiting for the dawn. Several times his called one of his soldiers. "Any word from Elizabeth?" he asked.

The answer was the same, "No."

Before dawn he gathered his soldiers in a field near the tents.

The sky was dark as Graham placed his soldiers facing the east. He rode before them and he counted his men. He had less than five hundred.

More than five hundred soldiers deserted. The soldiers were told the angel of God was coming to deliver the boy and the monks. Many soldiers dropped their weapons and they ran from the camp. The soldiers were afraid.

Graham and his remaining soldiers waited for the angel of God. They faced the east as the first rays of the sun lit the sky.

To the east they saw a mist forming. The mist was like fog but the mist was not fog. The mist became very thick. Slowly, the mist thinned. A man on a white horse rode through the mist toward them. The man and his horse stopped before them.

The soldiers gasped and they dropped their weapons. The soldiers fell to their knees onto the ground.

Graham could see him. Where the mist formed was the angel of God.

He was larger than any soldier Graham had seen. The angel of God sat on a white horse. His horse was white like the clouds.

His breastplate was of gold and silver and upon his head was a helmet of gold and silver. His hair was of dark black and his beard was of dark black. His eyes were as fire.

Graham could see the angel carried no shield. Graham looked at the hilt of his sword. The hilt of his sword was of gold.

The angel of God spoke and his voice boomed at them, "God commands you set these people free!"

Graham replied, "We mean them no harm."

The angel of God pulled his sword from its sheath. The sword burned with white fire. He held the sword of white fire in the air. The white fire covered the sword, the angel of God, and his horse.

Graham held his hand up and he quickly spoke, "Wait!"

The angel of God did not move or speak.

Graham ordered, "Bring them here! Bring everyone here!"

Several soldiers ran to the stockade and they opened the gate.

One soldier spoke to the monks, "Come quickly! The angel of God is before us."

The soldiers ran to the tent of Timothy.

The monks quickly stood. The monks picked up several boxes and they followed the soldiers to Timothy's tent.

The soldiers entered Timothy's tent. One soldier spoke, "Come quickly! The angel of God is before us."

Timothy, his mother, and his father went to where Graham sat on his horse. The monks followed Timothy. The monks carried several boxes with them.

Graham spoke to Timothy, "Is this a trick? Is this the angel of God who has been sent to deliver you?"

Timothy looked at the angel of God.

Timothy looked at Graham and he said, "God does not play tricks. Before you is the angel of God Jaykal."

Graham asked, "What will he do?"

Timothy replied, "If it is God's will he will destroy you and all who stand with you."

"If it is God's will he will destroy England."

Graham yelled to the angel Jaykal, "I obey God's command. I set these people free."

The angel Jaykal did not move. He held his sword of white fire in the air.

Graham spoke to Timothy, "Quickly, leave."

"I meant you no harm. I only wanted to save England."

Timothy looked at Graham. He said, "You did."

Timothy and the others walked toward the angel Jaykal. As they approached the angel, they bowed before him.

The angel Jaykal did not move. He sat upon his horse holding his sword of white fire in the air.

Timothy and the others walked quickly past the angel Jaykal to the border of Scotland.

The angel Jaykal did not move.

רבקה

When they crossed the English border, the angel Jaykal returned his sword to its sheath. The white fire left the angel Jaykal and his horse.

Then, the mist began to come. The mist became very thick. Slowly, the mist thinned. When the mist thinned, the angel Jaykal was not there.

The soldiers rose from their knees. They looked at Graham. One soldier asked, "Who were those monks? What do they carry?"

Graham spoke, "Timothy gathered monks from England, Scotland, Ireland, France, and Spain. Those monks can read and write many languages. Within the boxes they carry the word of God."

The soldier asked, "What word?"

Graham spoke, "They carry scrolls which have been written by many. The many will be joined as one."

Epilogue to Timothy

On July 24, 1567, Mary of Guise was forced to abdicate her throne to her 13 month-old son, James Charles Stuart. Mary of Guise was known as "Mary Queen of Scots." Her son James was crowned King James VI of Scotland.

Queen Elizabeth I of England died in 1603. At her death, King James VI of Scotland became ruler of Scotland, England, and Ireland. He was crowned King James I. His kingdom was referred to as, "Great Britain."

In 1604, King James I commissioned a new translation of the Bible. A team of more than 50 linguists and translators were chosen to prepare the new Bible.

At the time the team formed, many boxes were delivered to the Jerusalem Chamber of the Westminster Abbey. These boxes contained many scrolls and their translations. The scrolls were said to have been gathered together from many parts of the world. The scrolls were said to have been taken to Scotland where they were translated.

The scrolls were said to be divinely written and divinely translated.

The task of the commission was completed in the year 1610. It took one year to print the results. In the year 1611, The King James Version of the Holy Bible was authorized and released.

The King James Version of the Holy Bible is the greatest piece of literature ever written.

Elizabeth

Eric looked out of the window. The priest and the others were walking toward the gate. Eric noticed a man, woman, and a young boy near the gate. They were sitting under a tree in the shade. As the priest approached, they stood and kneeled to the priest. The priest made the sign of the cross to them.

Eric asked Irene, "Who are those people by the gate? Are they relatives?"

Irene came to the window and she looked out. "I'm not sure who the man and woman are. The boy's name is Antonio. They arrived late yesterday and my father spoke to them. It seems the young boy wants to see Elizabeth. He also wants to talk to us alone. He says he has something to tell us," Irene said.

Eric asked, "Who is he?"

Irene responded, "I do not know. My father said the man told him they came from San Marino. The boy told my father he was told Elizabeth was ill."

Eric asked, "I am not familiar with Italy. Where is San Marino?"

Irene answered, "It's about two hundred maybe three hundred miles from here. It's on the eastern coast."

Eric said, "That's a long way. How did they get here?"

Irene stopped looking out the window. She turned to Eric and said, "That's the strange part. It seems they walked."

"Walked? What do you mean walked? They walked three hundred miles?" Eric asked.

"The man told my father they received a few rides but mainly they walked here from San Marino," Irene said.

"Why?" Eric asked.

"The boy says he wants to see Elizabeth. He says he needs to speak to us alone. He has something to tell us. He also told my father to tell us something else," Irene said.

"What is that?" Eric asked.

"The boy told my father to tell us that everything is going to be OK. God is protecting Elizabeth," Irene said.

"What is this about?" Eric asked.

"It's a Catholic thing. These people hear about a sickness or a death and they come to offer their prayers. They are very sincere. They offer to light candles at the church. Then, they ask for money for the candles. Of course, you give them money," Irene said.

"Then what?" Eric asked.

"They say their prayers and light the candles at the church. You give them more money than the candles cost. They use the extra money for food," Irene replied.

"So, this young boy Antonio wants to say his prayers for Elizabeth?" Eric asked.

"I'm sure of it. He may want to join the priesthood," she replied.

"What does he want to tell us that no one should listen?" Eric asked.

"Who knows?" Irene shrugged her shoulders. "He probably wants to give his sincere prayer to us. He may feel that if he speaks in private, his prayers have more meaning," Irene answered.

"Is he OK?" Eric asked.

"Yes. He is with his mother and father. They arrived last night and he has waited by the gate. He has manners because he asked to speak to my father. He asked my father's permission to speak to us," she added.

"Do you really think they came three hundred miles?" Eric asked.

"It's possible. These people hear about such things and they come great distances. It is a part of their religion," Irene answered.

"How much money do we have?" Eric asked.

"Don't worry about the money. Dad gave them food last night and this morning. Dad feels honored that they are here. Dad will take care of them," Irene said.

"Tell your father to send him in," Eric said.

Irene went to the opened door and she called for her father. Her father Angelo came to the door and Irene spoke to him in Italian. Eric did not understand one word but he saw Angelo nod his head. Angelo then came into the room and he made the sign of the cross over Elizabeth's bed. He bent down and kissed her on the forehead. Then, he left the room.

Eric went to the window and he watched the three people by the gate. He saw Angelo go to the young boy and speak to him. The young boy said something to his parents and then he followed Angelo.

Eric began to think of the last week. So much happiness and so much sadness. He turned and looked at Elizabeth. She was lying in her bed asleep. She was so beautiful. Her dark hair was a contrast to her white baptism gown. There was sweat on her forehead from the fever.

Elizabeth had contracted meningitis. She would live perhaps days or maybe a few weeks.

Eric walked to her bed. He wiped her forehead with a linen cloth. He then bent over and he kissed her cheek gently.

She had slept through the baptism. Irene's parents insisted that Elizabeth be baptized before she died. They believe she will not enter heaven unless she is baptized.

Irene did not tell her parents that she had left the Catholic Church. Irene was baptized in the Baptist Church several months ago in Chicago. Eric and Irene argued over Elizabeth's baptism in the Catholic Church. Eric was against it but he finally agreed.

Eric wanted to take Elizabeth back to the United States for treatment. The doctor said, 'No." Elizabeth would not survive the trip home. Elizabeth would die in Italy. They decided to bury her here. Her grave would be located in the cemetery near the church.

רבקה

The white dress she was baptized in would be her burial dress. The doctor said she may last a few more days, maybe a week. There is nothing they can do.

Eric asked himself, 'How can you squeeze fifty, sixty, or seventy years into a few days? How can you squeeze days into hours?'

Eric answered himself, 'You can't.'

Eric wanted to cry but he couldn't. He had no tears left.

The door to their bedroom opened.

"Eric, meet Antonio," Irene said, as she and Antonio entered the room.

Eric looked at Antonio. He was about eight years old. He was dressed very shabby. The first thought in Eric's mind was he must come from a rural area. Antonio's father was probably a hired worker. Antonio smiled a big grin as he saw Eric.

"Hello, Antonio," Eric replied.

Irene translated Eric's English into Italian. Antonio smiled at Eric and he looked at Elizabeth. He said something in Italian.

Irene said, "His dialect is different. I'm not sure where he's from. Even my father had some trouble understanding him. He said, 'Do not worry. God is with Elizabeth."

Irene closed the door.

She said, "He told me that he has something to tell us which no one but us can hear. He said he was told about Elizabeth several days ago. He traveled as fast as possible."

Antonio watched Irene close the door. He looked around the room and he could see we were the only ones there. He looked at Elizabeth and then he looked at Irene and Eric. Then he began speaking.

Eric could not understand one word. He looked at Irene's face. She had many different expressions.

Antonio quit speaking. Eric asked Irene, "What did he say?"

Irene motioned for Eric to be quite.

Antonio began to speak again.

Eric watched Irene's face. Her face turned almost white.

Antonio held out his arms.

"What does he want?" Eric asked.

Irene looked at Eric. "He asked permission to hold Elizabeth," Irene replied.

"What?" Eric asked.

"It's OK. He will not hurt her," Irene replied.

Antonio held out his arms.

Irene reached into Elizabeth's bed and she picked up Elizabeth. Elizabeth was awakened and she began to cry.

"Is she OK?" Eric asked.

"Everything's OK," Irene said.

She handed Elizabeth to Antonio.

Antonio held Elizabeth close. He whispered into her ear and Elizabeth stopped crying.

Antonio said something.

"What did he say?" Eric asked.

"Not now, later," Irene said.

Antonio waved his hand over Elizabeth's body. He looked up and he said something.

Antonio spoke again. Then, he handed Elizabeth to Irene.

Antonio spoke again and Elizabeth bowed to Antonio.

Irene looked at Eric. "Bow!" she said.

Eric did not know what was going on but he bowed anyway.

Antonio turned and he opened the door. Antonio left the room.

"What was that all about?" Eric asked.

Irene was pale. She laid Elizabeth in her bed. She then went to the opened door and she called for her father. Her father came to the door and she spoke to him in Italian. Eric understood two words. He understood Antonio's name and another name, Rebecca.

When Irene said "Rebecca" her father repeated the word several times. He then went to Elizabeth's bed and he kneeled before Elizabeth's bed. He made the sign of the cross. Angelo said something in Italian. Eric heard him say the word Rebecca.

Angelo left the room in a hurry.

"What's going on? Where's Angelo running? What did Antonio say?" Eric asked.

"I'll tell you in a few minutes," Irene said.

She ran to Elizabeth's bed and she picked up Elizabeth.

"Her fever's gone!" she cried.

"What?" Eric said.

Eric ran to Irene and he took Elizabeth from her. Elizabeth was not hot. She felt normal and she was awake.

"What happened?" Eric asked.

"Who was this kid? Why did we bow?" Eric added.

"He was a messenger and he delivered a gift, " Irene said.

"What are you talking about? Who is Rebecca?" Eric asked.

Suddenly, Angelo came into the room. He spoke very quickly in Italian. Then, Angelo looked at Eric. Eric was holding Elizabeth.

Angelo said something else in Italian. Angelo kneeled before Eric and he made the sign of the cross. Angelo reached up and he pressed Elizabeth's hand against his forehead.

Irene spoke to her father in Italian. He father shook his head no several times. Then, he bowed his head and he shook his head yes.

Angelo said something else in Italian. He stood up and he left the room. However, he backed out of the room. His eyes never left Elizabeth.

"What did he say? What's going on?" Eric asked.

"I sent my father to find Antonio. I asked my father to give Antonio and his parents anything they wish. My father searched for Antonio and he is gone. I also asked my father to send for the doctor. The doctor will be here tomorrow," Irene said.

"The doctor! Elizabeth looks fine. Why did you send for the doctor?" Eric asked.

"To prove what I know," said Irene.

"What's that?" asked Eric.

"I want the doctor to prove that Elizabeth is OK," said Irene.

"OK! You think she is OK?" asked Eric.

"I don't think, I know. Do you know who Antonio is? Do you know why we bowed to him?" asked Irene.

"I do not know. Who is he and who is Rebecca?" asked Eric.

Irene said, "My grandfather told us a story which his grandfather told him. The story is older than the New Testament. The story is about an infant child named Rebecca. God healed Rebecca through the apostle Simon Peter. God gave Rebecca a gift. This gift from God was that God healed through the hands of Rebecca."

"When Rebecca reached a certain age, God took the gift from Rebecca and God gave the gift to another child. God took the gift from that child and God gave the gift to another child. God has passed the gift from child to child."

"Antonio had the gift from God. God sent Antonio to Elizabeth and God healed Elizabeth through the hands of Antonio. God passed the gift from Antonio to Elizabeth."

"God has healed Elizabeth and Elizabeth is blessed by God. God will heal through the hands of Elizabeth."

Eric asked, "So, that is what Antonio said?"

"That's not all. Antonio said something I have not heard. Antonio said, 'It is the will of God that for generations to come all will know the power of God through the hands of a child. God will heal Elizabeth through my hands and God will heal no other through my hands. What was given to me will be taken from me. What was taken from me will be given to Elizabeth. God will heal through the hands of Elizabeth."

'Elizabeth is protected by God himself. No man, woman, child, or beast of the earth shall harm her. This is the will of God."

He also said, 'Your daughter Elizabeth will serve God. Return to your place and share the blessing which God has given," Irene said.

Eric said, "Irene, this is just a story your grandfather told you. I have not heard of Rebecca or anything like it."

"Just because you have not heard it does not make it false. We have heard the story of Rebecca and we believe it, " Irene said.

"What was this between you and your father?" Eric asked.

"I made my father swear before God that he would not reveal what Antonio said and what has been done. My father agreed. He will tell no one. He will not even tell my mother," Irene said.

"You mean we can't tell anyone?" asked Eric.

"No one is to know, "said Irene.

"So what does this mean?" Eric asked.

"It means we follow the will of God, " Irene added.

"When does all this begin?" Eric asked.

"It's already begun. It began when God passed the gift from Antonio to Elizabeth, " Irene said.

Eric looked at Elizabeth. She didn't look different. Well, she did look different. She didn't look sick. Her fever was gone and she was active.

Elizabeth seemed OK. She ate fine and she soiled a few diapers. Irene took the baptism dress off and she bathed her. She looked and acted like she did before she got sick. Elizabeth was walking and jabbering. It was like a miracle.

It was late in the day and Eric and Irene had supper. They ate at the table and Angelo looked at Elizabeth strangely. Angelo would not take his eyes off of Elizabeth.

After supper, they decided to take a nap.

They lay on the bed. Then, Angelo knocked on their door.

Angelo came into the room and he acted strange. He kneeled before Elizabeth and he placed her hand on his forehead. He said something in Italian and then he left. When Angelo left, he again backed out of the room. He did not take his eyes off of Elizabeth.

Eric asked, "What did he say?"

"It's started," said Irene.

"What's started?" asked Eric.

"There's a woman outside with three children. She has asked to see Elizabeth," Irene said.

"What do you mean? She has asked to see Elizabeth," Eric said.

My father said, 'There is a woman with three children outside. The woman heard of a child healed by God and blessed by God. She has brought her children to be blessed."

Eric was angry. He said, "Irene, your father told this story and now people are believing it."

Irene said, "No Eric. My father has told no one. He has never seen this woman. This woman said she has traveled two days to get here. One of her children is crippled. She was praying in church when a voice told her to come here. She doesn't know my father."

"Come on Irene! This is silly. If this story is true, how could this woman know God passed the gift from Antonio to Elizabeth two days ago? All this happened this morning after the baptism," Eric said.

"I don't know, " said Irene.

"Where is she?" asked Eric.

"She's at the gate. She told my father she is not worthy to enter Holy ground. God dwells in this house with Elizabeth," Irene said.

Eric went to the window and he looked out. He could see a woman and three small children standing near the gate. Angelo was speaking to them.

"This is silly. Tell your father to bring them in. I will talk to them," Eric said.

Irene opened the window and she yelled to her father in Italian. Her father spoke to the woman and then he yelled back to Irene.

Irene said, "My father said the woman will not come in. She will not pass the gate for it is Holy ground. God dwells in this house with Elizabeth."

Irene's father yelled to her in Italian.

"What did he say?" Eric asked.

Irene said, "He asked us to bring Elizabeth to the gate. The woman will not leave until they have asked God's blessing through the child."

Eric was very irritated. "OK. Let's go to the gate," he said.

Eric and Irene wrapped Elizabeth in a blanket. It wasn't cold but Eric insisted that they wrap her up. He was afraid she would get sick again.

They went to the gate and the woman and her three children bowed before them. Eric looked at the children. There were dressed very shabby. They looked like they have not eaten well in a long time. The mother looked very old but she was young. He felt very sad for them.

Irene's father said something in Italian. The woman looked at Angelo and she lined her three children in front of her.

Angelo said something to Irene in Italian.

Irene said, "My father asks that we place Elizabeth before them that they may ask for God's blessing."

Eric stood Elizabeth in front of the gate.

The woman and her three children kneeled. The woman said something in Italian.

Then, something happened.

Elizabeth stood in front of the gate. She did not move, speak, or make one sound. Elizabeth stood like she knew everything that was going on.

Elizabeth looked at the crippled child. The child was a girl. She was about six years old. Her left leg looked like it was bent. She had a covering on her foot where she dragged her leg to walk.

Elizabeth looked at the girl and Elizabeth held her hand out toward the girl.

The young girl stood and she walked toward Elizabeth. The young girl dragged her foot as she walked. She kneeled before Elizabeth.

She said something in Italian and she took Elizabeth's hand and she pressed it to her forehead. The young girl released Elizabeth's hand.

Elizabeth placed her hand on the girl's head.

Then, a miracle happened.

The young girl's leg twisted.

Eric quickly grabbed Elizabeth and he ran into the house. Eric ran to their room and he looked out the window. The woman was bowing toward the house.

He could see Irene and Angelo speaking to the woman. The woman was bowing and the three kids were bowing. The woman made the sign of the cross and they began to walk away. Eric looked at the crippled girl as she walked away. She was no longer dragging her foot. Eric saw Irene run toward the house.

Irene came running into the room. "It's true!" she said.

"God healed the girl. The mother asked for God's blessing and the girl asked for God's blessing. God healed the girl through Elizabeth's hands," Irene added.

"Something happened. That girl's leg twisted like butter," Eric said.

"Where is your father?" Eric asked.

"He went to get them food. They are waiting beyond the gate. Eric, I don't think they have eaten in two days," Irene replied.

"How did this woman know about Elizabeth? I mean, she said she has been traveling for two days," Eric said.

Irene responded, "My father said she told him that she was praying in church and a voice spoke to her. The voice told her that there is a child healed by God and blessed by God. The voice said she is to take her children and seek the child. When they come before the child, her daughter is to ask for God's blessing. She is to touch the child and the child will touch her. God will heal her daughter through the hands of the child."

"How did they know to come here? The woman does not know your father," Eric said.

"The woman told my father that the voice said it will guide her to the child," Irene said.

Eric shook his head. "Man! Oh, man!" he said.

Eric looked at Elizabeth. She was playing with a small stuffed bear she owned. Elizabeth didn't look different. She looked like an average fourteen-month old child.

Eric heard Irene's father speaking as he came into the room. This time, Angelo bowed before he entered the room. He said something in Italian and then he spoke to Irene.

Irene nodded her head and then Angelo left. Again, he backed out of the room. He never took his eyes off of Elizabeth.

Irene spoke, "My father said everything is OK. He gave the woman some food and money. She understands that God sent her to the child. God will send others. She is not to reveal where the child is."

"Others? What do you mean others?" Eric asked.

"God will send many to Elizabeth and God will send Elizabeth to many," Irene said.

"When will this end?" Eric asked.

"One day, God will send Elizabeth to a child. God will heal that child through Elizabeth's hands and God will take the gift from Elizabeth and give the gift to another. God will no longer heal through Elizabeth's hands," Irene said.

"That part will end. We will always follow God's will," she added.

Eric, Irene, and Elizabeth stayed at Irene's family home for several weeks. During those weeks, many people came to the home to see the child healed by God and blessed by God.

These people asked for God's blessing and they touched Elizabeth and Elizabeth touched them. God healed all who touched Elizabeth and were touched by her.

One day, God spoke to Eric in prayer and God told Eric to return to his place. Eric, Irene, and Elizabeth returned to America.

For as spoken by young Antonio, 'Your daughter Elizabeth will serve God. Return to your place and share the blessing which God has given."

Ebet

The man walked into the restaurant. He looked around the room until he saw the person he was looking for. A young man sat at a table near the window. The young man was reading the newspaper.

The man walked to the table. "Hello, Tom," he said.

Tom responded, "Well Sam. What's the latest story?

Sam sat down. "Were looking for a dog. Do you want to hear the sane part or the crazy part?" Sam asked.

"Which part will I believe?" asked Tom.

"Neither," replied Sam.

"Well. Tell me the sane part and then tell me the crazy part," Tom laughed.

"They are both kind of mixed. You can't tell the sane without jumping to the crazy," Sam said.

"Is this something I should write down? Is there a front page story here?" Tom asked.

"There is a bunch of something but I don't think your editor would print it. I will tell you the sane part first and then I will tell you the crazy part," Sam said.

"I'm listening," said Tom.

"Yesterday a pit pull broke his chain over on the south side. The pit bull wandered into a yard and scared three kids pretty bad. The kids are still shook up," Sam said.

"OK. Are the three kids OK?" asked Tom.

"Yes. The three kids are OK, I guess. The pit bull didn't hurt them but the kids are pretty messed up in the head. They are saying strange things," Sam said.

"OK." Tom said. "Where is the sane part?" he added.

"That's it. Everything after that is crazy," Sam said.

"What do you mean that's the sane part?" Tom asked.

"That's it. That is the only part of the story that's sane. Everything else is crazy," Sam said.

"What happened to the pit bull?" Tom asked.

"We don't know. We can't find him. Animal control has been searching since yesterday. They are still searching. No one has seen the dog and no one has reported seeing the dog," Sam said.

Tom asked again, "What happened to the pit bull?"

"Are you ready for the crazy?" Sam asked.

Tom said, "Sure."

"God destroyed the pit bull in white fire," Sam said.

"White fire! God destroyed the dog! Where did this come from?" Tom asked.

"The three kids. The kids claim God destroyed the pit bull with white fire," Sam said.

"What a story. No wonder it's a crazy," Tom laughed.

Sam leaned forward and he spoke very abruptly, "It's not funny! No one is laughing! You have to hear the whole story."

"Well. Tell me the story?" Tom asked.

Sam spoke, "Yesterday, we received a 911 call that a dog had attacked another dog and four children."

Tom said, "Wait one minute. I thought there were three children. Where did the fourth child come from?"

Sam added, "That's a part of the crazy."

Tom said, "Continue."

Sam continued, "A cruiser responded to the 911 call. The officer found three kids frantic. He also found an older dog, a female chow named Ginger, with blood all over her. The kids claimed a pit bull attacked Ginger and they tried to fight the dog."

"That is the only thing we have been able to verify."

"This pit bull breaks his chain. The pit bull is several blocks from where these kids are playing and the pit bull wanders to where the kids are playing. The three kids are playing in their yard. In the yard is this plastic house. You have probably seen one. The house looks like a log cabin."

Tom nodded yes.

"These kids are playing in the plastic house. They call it their fort. One of the kids lives here and he has an older dog, named Ginger. Ginger is a sort of chow mixed. Anyway, Ginger is chained to her dog house and these kids are playing."

"The kids hear Ginger howl. They look out of this plastic house to see the pit bull tearing into this older dog."

"Well, the kids start screaming at the pit bull and then they start throwing things at the pit bull. One of the kids hits the pit bull with a rock. Well, the pit bull stops biting Ginger and the pit bull stares at the three kids."

"All hell breaks lose."

"The kids are screaming and trying to hide in the plastic house. Ginger is howling from where the pit bull was biting her. The pit bull is getting ready to charge the three kids. Then, the fourth kid appears out of nowhere."

Tom gulped, "Out of nowhere?"

"I get it," Tom said, "It's a ghost story. This fourth kid is a ghost."

"The fourth kid is no ghost. As far as we know the fourth kid is alive and well," Sam said.

"Well how old is this kid?" asked Tom.

"Are you ready for the crazy?" Sam asked.

"The crazy! It's crazy already. These kids survived the attack of a pit bull?" Tom asked.

"The pit bull never touched the three kids. The three kids are fine. Not one scratch," Sam said.

"What happened to the pit bull?" asked Tom.

"This kid that appeared from nowhere is a neighborhood kid. The kid is about two years old. Her name is Ebet," Sam said.

"Two years old! The pit bull attacked the two year old! My God, destroy that dog! " Tom shouted.

"The pit bull didn't hurt the two year old," said Sam.

"Thank God!" said Tom.

"Did someone kill the dog?" Tom asked.

"No. We don't think so. We haven't found the pit bull. We do not know if the dog is alive or dead. Animal control is still looking for him," Sam said.

"Man! Talk about crazy! So, what happened?" Tom asked.

"Well. We have Ginger howling in pain. We have these three kids yelling for Ebet to run to the fort. We have this pit bull staring at Ebet and Ebet is between the three kids and the pit bull," Sam said.

Tom took a drink of coffee. "What happened?" Tom gulped.

"The crazy begins," said Sam.

"The pit bull charges the two year old girl. And according to the three kids, Ebet catches on fire," said Sam.

"Fire! These kids were playing with matches? Did you arrest their parents?" Tom asked.

Sam spoke, "No. The kids were not playing with matches. They said Ebet was covered with white fire."

"The pit bull jumps Ebet and the pit bull is covered with white fire," Sam added.

"What happened to Ebet? " Tom asked.

"Nothing. According to the three kids, the pit bull disappeared. The white fire left Ebet," Sam said.

"What? This is crazy. How old are these kids?" Tom asked.

"Well, the three kids are like five, six, and seven," Sam said.

"These kids are watching too much TV. No wonder the story is crazy. So what happened?" asked Tom.

"I'm telling you what the kids said. Ebet was standing between the pit bull and them. The three kids are screaming for Ebet to run to the fort. The pit bull charged Ebet and suddenly Ebet was covered with white fire. The pit bull jumped her and the pit bull was covered with white fire. Then, the pit bull disappeared," said Sam.

"Oh, yeah," Tom said.

"Then, the white fire left Ebet. Are you ready for the next crazy?" Sam asked.

"Next crazy! How much crazier can it get?" Tom asked.

"Real crazy. The kids said Ebet went to Ginger. Here is this older dog howling because this pit bull chewed her up. The little girl lays on top of Ginger and Ginger stops howling. Then, Ginger gets up like nothing is wrong," said Sam.

"What?" Tom asked.

"Ebet's parents suddenly appear. And get this. According to the three kids, the parents went straight to them. They never even looked at their daughter," Sam said.

"Oh, man. What a low life," Tom said.

"Yeah. Tell me about it. Anyway, Ebet's parents are more concerned with the three kids then their own daughter. The three kids are screaming about this pit bull and Ebet's father tells the kids that God destroyed the dog. The dog is gone!" Sam said.

"What a crock," Tom said.

"Then, Ebet's parents took their little girl and left," Sam said.

"Well! Did you arrest them? They deserve to be arrested. Hay, what happened to the pit bull?" asked Tom.

"More crazy coming up," Sam said.

"At this time, the kids run into the house screaming about this pit bull. One of the parents comes out to the yard and there is blood all over Ginger. The parent called in a 911. The squad car was there in about six minutes," Sam said.

"What about Ebet?" Tom asked.

Sam said, "Well, that is part of the crazy. It seems that Ebet is a former neighbor. The little girl lived about three houses down the street. The family moved about two weeks ago."

"The family moved somewhere east. They had a yard sale and sold most of their stuff. Ebet's father had a big going away party where he worked and the family moved. No one has seen the family since these three kids claim to have seen them."

"What? This is crazy," said Tom.

"It gets crazier," Sam said.

"It seems one of the kids, the girl, saw Ebet and her parents earlier in the day. They were walking in front of the house where this whole thing occurred. The kid said she waved to them and they waved back. She didn't think anything about it. The kid said they looked like they were waiting for something. She thought they came to see her parents," Sam said.

Sam added, "Anyway, there is blood all over Ginger but the dog is not bleeding. So, one of the units took the dog to the vet to be checked."

"In the event the child was there and did get hurt, we called the hospital. The officer asked the emergency room if a two-year old girl had been brought to the hospital with possible dog bites. The officer was on hold for about ten minutes. Then, a doctor took the telephone. The doctor wanted a description of the little girl," Sam said.

"So, she was hurt. Man, this ticks me off," said Tom.

Sam said, "No. No little girl had been brought to the hospital but the doctor wanted to know what she looked like."

"What does she look like?" asked Tom.

"Well, she is petite. Weighs about thirty pounds. She has an olive complexion with shoulder length brown hair," Sam said.

Sam added, "Then, the doctor wanted a detective to come to the hospital."

"What?" Tom asked.

"Then, the vet called. The vet wanted an officer to come to his clinic," Sam added.

"What? This is getting crazy," Tom said.

"Are you ready for the big crazy?" Sam asked.

"There's more?" asked Tom.

"Much more," said Sam.

Sam started to speak when a detective named Alex walked to the table. Alex interrupted Sam.

"Sorry Sam. Chief needs to talk to you. He sent me to find you. Call him now," Alex said.

Sam stood up. "I'll be back in a minute," he said.

Alex sat down beside Tom.

"Well, from the look on your face Sam is telling you about the pit bull," Alex said.

Tom said, "Yeah. A real crazy story."

"How far has he got?" Alex asked.

"He was going to tell me about the hospital," Tom said.

"Heard about the vet yet?" Alex asked.

"No. Not yet," Tom said.

"Hay! What is this all about? Some ghost kid?" Tom asked.

"I wish it was a ghost. If the kid was a ghost it would make sense," Alex said.

"What happened? What really happened?" Tom asked.

"My opinion and off the record?" Alex asked.

"Yeah, sure," said Tom.

"Well, we know for a fact that a pit bull broke lose. We spoke to the owner. The dog was a mean one. I figure a car hit the dog and the dog was hurt and bleeding. The dog wandered into the yard where the kids were playing. Then, the pit bull attacked the older dog - that's where the blood came from. The kids scared the dog away and the dog is lying somewhere under a bush or a house dead. That's my opinion," said Alex.

"What about this little girl, the little girl named Ebet? " asked Tom.

"The kid is gone. The family moved away about two weeks ago. These kids are kids. These kids believe in the tooth fairy and they think Barney is a real dinosaur. Wake up Tom," Alex said.

"What about this other stuff that Sam is going to tell me?" Tom asked.

"Judge for yourself. Anyway, here comes Sam. The chief was really hot to talk to him," Alex said.

Sam sat down and he took a drink of water.

"Well, more crazy," Sam said.

"What?" asked Tom.

Sam said, "Later. Where was I? Oh, the vet. Anyway, an officer went to see the vet. It seems that this vet has been taking care of Ginger since she was a pup. The vet checked Ginger and he could not find any wounds. There was blood and saliva on the dog."

"The vet took several x-rays. While he was waiting for them to develop, he checked the blood on the dog. The blood was animal, not human."

"So, what is the big deal?" Tom asked.

"The vet claims that this dog is not Ginger," Sam said.

"What?" asked Tom.

Sam said, "It seems that Ginger wandered into the street when she was a pup and she was struck by a car. Ginger's left front leg was broken. The vet set the leg. It also seems that someone closed a door on her tail and her tail was broken. Ginger's tail had a small crook. It also seems that Ginger has some sort of hip problem."

"Well, the x-rays show no sign of a broken leg or a broken tail. Also, the x-rays show no sign of a hip problem. The doctor thinks this dog is a sibling of Ginger."

"That's crazy," Tom said.

"Yeah. I think so too. I think the vet has got his dogs mixed up," Tom said.

"What about the doctor at the hospital?" Tom asked.

Alex interrupted, "This is the good one."

"Yes, this is the good one," Sam said.

Sam added, "There is a young boy at the hospital. The boy's name is Tommy. Tommy is eight years old. Tommy had been sick and his doctor ordered tests. It seems the boy had leukemia."

"Had leukemia? What do you mean, had?" asked Tom.

Sam continued, "The day before all of this happened, a man, women, and a two year old girl visited Tommy in the hospital. The man asked Tommy if he believed in God. Tommy said, 'Yes." Then, the man asked Tommy if he believed God could do anything. Tommy said, 'Yes." Then, the man asked Tommy if he believed God could heal him. Tommy again said, 'Yes." Then, the man told Tommy to ask for God's blessing and touch the little girl. Tommy asked for God's blessing and he touched the little girl. Then, the little girl touched Tommy. Tommy said he felt funny. Then, the man told him that God had healed him."

"What a creep," Tom said.

"Yeah. Tommy told his parents about this man and they were furious. The hospital staff looked for the three people but they couldn't find them. The only way they could calm Tommy was to tell him it was dream," Sam said.

"OK. Where's the crazy other than this loon scaring the kid," Tom asked.

"Well, that's the crazy. Tommy no longer has leukemia," Sam said.

"What? The doctor must have made a mistake," Tom said.

"No mistake. Several doctors looked at the early tests. Tommy had leukemia. And that's not all," Sam said.

"What do you mean?" asked Tom.

"It seems two other people in the hospital had the same thing happen to them. One man had several arteries blocked and one woman had severe kidney problems. They both claim a man, woman, and a two-year old girl visited them. The man asked them the same questions he asked Tommy. They asked for God's blessing and they touched the little girl. The little girl touched them. They both said they felt funny."

"The man told them that God had healed them," Sam said.

"Well! Are they healed?" asked Tom.

"Yes. They are both healthy," Sam added.

"Is this little girl, Ebet?" asked Tom.

"That is the ten million dollar question. The answer is no," Sam said.

"What do you mean no?" asked Tom.

"Well, Ebet has been gone for two weeks. No one in the neighborhood has seen her or her parents since they moved. She fits the description of the little girl but sixty percent of the two year old girls in America probably fit the description," Sam added.

"So, what do you know about this little girl named Ebet?" asked Tom.

Sam said, "That is Alex's department.

Sam looked at Alex and he said, "Tell him what you found."

Alex said, "All we have so far is what was told to the neighbors. It seems the Browns moved here about two months ago. They moved here from Chicago. Mr. Brown met the future Mrs. Brown at Chicago State. Mr. Brown was in advertising and the future Mrs. Brown was in art."

"They met, fell in love, got married, and the little Brown was born. It seems that Mrs. Brown is Italian. When the little Brown was about one year old, they visited Mrs. Brown's parents in Italy."

"The little Brown got sick in Italy. It seems she contracted meningitis. The little girl almost died."

"How sick was she?" asked Tom.

"Sick enough that they began to make funeral arrangements. They were going to bury her in Italy. Then, she suddenly got better. They stayed in Italy a few months then they returned to Chicago," Alex said.

Alex added, "Mr. Brown worked at a local company, the Bradford Company. The Bradford Company makes custom T-shirts, coffee mugs, etc. He was a good worker. He told his boss they were moving east."

"Well! Where did they go?" asked Tom.

"I don't know. We were told to drop it," said Alex.

"Why?" asked Tom.

"Nothing wrong here. Mr. Brown has no warrants or parking tickets. Mr. Brown has no problems with the law and the law has no problems with Mr. Brown. If we push it, it's an invasion of privacy. The matter is closed," Alex said.

"So, this is it?" Tom asked.

"I'm afraid so," said Alex.

"What about the story the kids told?" Tom asked.

"Oh, yes. That brings up my telephone call to the Captain," said Sam.

Sam added, "It seems the lady that was in the hospital, with the kidney problem, is Catholic. She told her priest that God healed her through the hands of a child. Her priest telephoned the hospital to ask about her illness and he was told about Tommy and the man with the heart condition. Her priest then heard the story of the pit bull and Ebet."

"Well, the priest started making telephone calls. I don't know who he called but last night the Captain received a telephone call from a priest. They spoke for a long time."

"This morning, the Captain received a call from another priest. It seems two priests are on their way here to interview the kids."

"Priests? Why are priests coming here?" Tom asked.

"Who knows," said Sam.

Sam added, "They are coming a long way. They are coming from Rome, Italy."

"Who are they?" asked Tom.

Sam looked at his notebook. He said, "The two priests are Father Mark and Father Robert. They should be here in two days. They left Rome last night."

Tom remarked, "All this way to hear three kids tell a crazy story about a two year old named Ebet."

"Oh, the kid's name is not Ebet," said Alex.

"What's her name?" asked Tom.

Alex said, "It seems these kids gave each other nicknames. Robert was called Berty. Tina was called Teen Teen. John was called Jo Jo. The dog Ginger had a nickname, Gin Gin. The little girl's name is Elizabeth, Elizabeth Brown. The kids called her Ebet."

Alex added, "We have the Brown family. Eric, Irene, and Elizabeth Brown are an average, ordinary family."

"So, what happens now?" asked Tom.

"Nothing. We continue looking for the pit bull. The vet is crazy. The doctor is crazy. Everyone is crazy except us," said Sam.

"What about the little girl at the hospital?" asked Tom.

"That is the real strange thing. The three people at the hospital said the man told them the little girl's name was Elizabeth," Alex said.

"Are you sure she's not the same girl?" asked Tom.

"Positive! Ebet's been gone for two weeks," Alex said.

"What about Tommy?" asked Tom.

"A miracle. Don't you believe in miracles Tom?" asked Alex.

"Yeah. If God healed Tommy, he did a first rate job," said Sam.

"What do you mean?" asked Tom.

Sam said, "It seems Tommy has worn glasses since he was about three. The kid looks like a frog staring through ice cubes. When he claimed God healed him, he had trouble seeing. The doctors thought his failing eyesight was a drug reaction. It seems the kid doesn't need glasses any more. He couldn't see through those thick glasses."

Alex broke in, "Don't forget about the teeth."

"Tommy had several cavities. The doctors were waiting for some test results before they allowed the dentist to fill the cavities. It seems Tommy has no cavities. God did a first rate job on Tommy. Not only did God cure the leukemia, God fixed his eyes and his teeth while he was at it," Sam said.

"What about the two priests?" Tom asked.

"What about them?" Sam remarked.

"Well! Are you going to talk to them? Are you going to tell them what you know?" asked Tom.

Sam said, "There's nothing to tell. Do you want me to tell them that God performed five miracles?"

"What do you mean five miracles?" asked Tom.

"There's the three people in the hospital and then there's the three kids and Ginger," Sam said.

"I thought the kids and Ginger weren't hurt?" asked Tom.

Sam said, "The three kids weren't hurt. If you believe in miracles, God sent this little girl to save those three kids."

" If the story of the kids is true, that pit bull tore Ginger all to pieces. The pit bull would have killed those three kids. God sent the little girl to those three kids and God protected them through the little girl. God destroyed the pit bull in white fire before the pit bull could harm the three kids."

"God healed Ginger like he healed the three people at the hospital."

"What about Ebet? I mean what about Elizabeth?" asked Tom.

"I wouldn't worry about her. If God is healing people through her hands, it seems God himself is protecting her. God covered her in white fire to protect her from the pit bull. She stood between the pit bull and the three kids. The pit bull had to go through her to get to the kids."

"The pit bull was consumed in the fire of God when he touched the white fire which protected her," said Sam.

Tom asked, "If the story of the three kids is true, why didn't God just destroy the pit bull? Why did God send this little girl to protect those children? Why did God send this little girl to those three people in the hospital?"

Sam replied, "We are but men. We do not know of the will of God."

Alex interrupted, "We need to leave or we will be late."

Tom asked, "Late? Where are you going?"

"Were going to church," Sam said.

Tom asked, "You are going to church in the afternoon?"

Alex said, "St. Luke's has a mass at noon. There are about ten officers from the department going."

Tom asked Alex, "I thought you were Baptist?"

Alex replied, "I am. I have not been to church in several years. I'm taking my family this Sunday. I have a lot of catching up to do."

Sam said, "Me too. My family is Methodist. My wife and kids go to church every Sunday. I'm usually too tired or I have some excuse. I'm going back to church also."

Tom said, "This is great! What made you guys change?"

Alex said, "We see the bad and good in people everyday. We see miracles but we have not paid much attention to them. We have seen people turn their lives around. It is time for us to recognize what we see."

Sam asked, "Do you want to go with us?"

Tom said, "Sure. Let me pay my bill."

Tom looked at his bill and he left some money on the table. The three men walked to the door.

As the three men walked to the door, Tom looked at Sam.

"Where do you think she is? Where do you think Ebet is now?" asked Tom.

"Wherever God wants her to be," said Sam.

רבקה

רבקה
Rachel's Secret

The Search for Rachel

The moving van began to drive off.

The two girls waved goodbye to the drivers and they ran into the house.

There were boxes everywhere. The woman opened a box and the two girls ran past her laughing.

"Stop running," she said.

"Let them run," a man's voice came from the kitchen.

The two girls ran through the house. Suddenly, they stopped running.

One of the girls yelled, "Mom! Mom! We have company."

The man and woman went to the front door. The door was opened and they could see the street. A taxicab was stopped in front of their house.

Two men emerged from the taxi. They both wore black clothes and they both wore a white collar. One man looked young. The other man looked very old.

The woman said, "Priests? Why are priests coming here?"

The taxicab did not drive off. The driver turned off the engine.

The two men walked toward the open door. Suddenly, the older priest fell to the ground. He yelled, "She was here! She was here!"

The man quickly opened the door and he ran outside the house. "Is he OK? " he asked.

The older priest said, "She was here! She was here!"

"Help me get him inside," the young priest said.

The two men helped the older man get up. "Come inside and we will sit him down," the man said.

They helped the older priest inside the house. The man brought a dining table chair to him. They helped the older priest to sit in the chair.

"Thanks," the young priest said.

"I am Father Mark. This is Father Robert. Thanks again for your help," Father Mark said.

The man, his wife, and their two daughters looked at the two priests.

The man said, "I am Bob. This is my wife Sally and our daughters Betty and Sandra."

"Is something wrong?" he asked.

"No. There is nothing wrong. We are looking for a young girl. The girl is named Rachel. Do you know if a young girl named Rachel lived here?" asked Father Mark.

"No. We just moved in today. The van just left," Bob replied.

Bob added, "We are renting the house. It has been empty for several weeks. I don't know who lived here before."

Sally spoke, "The landlord said the previous tenants were Eric and Irene Allen. I don't know if they had any children."

Father Robert spoke, "The room! Take me to her room!"

Father Mark asked, "Do you know if there is a room in the house which may have been the room of a young girl?"

Sally spoke, "There is a bedroom which is painted a pastel color. I guess it may have been the room of a young girl. It's here." She pointed toward the hallway.

Bob and Father Mark helped Father Robert from the chair. They helped him to the room. Father Robert entered the room and he began to touch the walls.

"This was her room. She lived here," Father Robert said.

"This is getting spooky," Bob said.

"I think you need to leave," Bob added.

"It's OK," Father Mark said.

"Were looking for a young girl named Rachel who may have lived here," he added.

"Do you know of a young girl named Rachel?" Father Mark asked.

Betty said, "Mom. I know a Rachel. She went to our school. I don't where she lived."

"What do you know about her?" Father Mark asked.

"Nothing much. She started coming to our school a couple of months ago. She was quite. She left school a couple of weeks ago," Betty said.

"What did she talk about? What were her interests?" asked Father Mark.

Betty said, "The usual stuff. She was an ordinary kid."

Betty added, "She did have a real good friend, Laurie. They were real close. They ate lunch together and I think I saw them at a movie."

"Mom, you remember Laurie? Laurie Gibson."

Sally said, "Oh, yes. Laurie. Laurie was in a really bad traffic accident. Someone ran a stop sign and the car hit the side Laurie was riding in. The whole side of the car was smashed in. Laurie was hurt really bad. She's in the hospital."

"When did the accident happen?" Father Mark asked.

Sally replied, "Yesterday, I think. Or maybe it was the day before. Anyway, Laurie's older sister was driving. Her sister wasn't hurt only Laurie."

"She's at the hospital. You may want to speak to her. But if Rachel lived here the family left town several weeks ago. She probably doesn't know where she is."

רבקה

"Why do you want to find this girl? Is something wrong?" Bob asked.

Father Mark replied, "No. There is nothing wrong. This girl is special! Very special!"

Betty said, "I don't think this is the Rachel you are looking for. She was sorta ordinary. Rachel left school a couple of weeks ago. I think her father got a new job."

"What do you mean special?" Bob asked.

"God heals through the hands of the child," Father Mark said.

"Have you heard of anyone who was really sick and then they got better real fast?" Father Mark added.

"No. We just moved into this house. We lived a couple of miles from here and we needed more room for the girls. The only person I know who is sick is Laurie," Sally said.

"I have not heard of anything like that," added Sally.

"Bob, do you know Alex Simpson?" Father Mark asked.

Bob spoke, "No. I have never heard of him. Who is he?"

Father Mark said, "Alex Simpson had cancer. He was expected to die. Suddenly, he got better. Alex said God healed him through the hands of a young girl. The girl's name was Rachel."

Bob looked at Father Robert. Father Robert was touching the walls of the room.

"I think it is time for you to leave," Bob said.

"We will go," said Father Mark.

"What is this all about?" asked Sally.

Father Mark said, "Many years ago an archeological dig near the city of Jerusalem uncovered a jar which contained nine scrolls. The scrolls were taken to Father Robert. Father Robert read the scrolls and the scrolls told of a child healed by God and blessed by God. God heals through the hands of the child."

"Father Robert began looking for evidence that this story was true. He found a lot of evidence to support the story."

Sandra asked, "The Dead Sea scrolls?"

Father Mark replied, "No. These nine scrolls are not the Dead Sea scrolls. These scrolls were found in the valley of Gehenna. Gehenna is where the trash of Jerusalem was gathered and burned."

"When were the scrolls written?" asked Bob.

Father Mark said, "They were written shortly after Christ was resurrected."

"So, this child has lived almost two thousand years?" Bob asked.

"No. The child has not lived almost two thousand years. The child passed the gift of healing to another child. That child passed the gift to another child. The gift has been passed from child to child. Father Robert thinks Rachel is the current child," Father Mark said.

Sally said, "This sounds like a movie."

"What makes Father Robert think that Rachel is the current child?" asked Bob.

"The pattern is the same. A young child comes to a town and people who are sick are suddenly healed. The people who are healed claim God healed them through the hands of a child. Then, the child moves away," Father Mark said.

"Alex Simpson claims God healed him through the hands of a young girl named Rachel," Father Mark added.

Bob asked, "So, how long have you been looking for these children?"

Father Mark said, "The church has heard stories of such a child for hundreds of years. We believed these stories were fiction. It is only when the scrolls were discovered that we began to believe these stories may be fact. Father Robert read the scrolls and he has devoted his life to finding the child."

Bob asked, "So, this child is a saint?"

Father Mark said, "No. The child is not a saint. We do not know exactly what the child is or the mission of the child. We do not know how to describe the child."

"The story sounds good. It's a shame," said Bob.

"What is a shame?" asked Father Mark.

Bob said, "Father Robert believes the stories are true and he has devoted his life to finding the child. When he dies, it's all over."

"It's not over," Father Mark said.

"I have devoted my life to finding the child. I will replace Father Robert."

Bob asked, "What are you going to do when you find the child?"

"I don't know," replied Father Mark.

Father Mark handed a card to Bob and he said, "If you hear of a person who is sick and suddenly healed, call me."

Bob helped Father Mark take Father Robert to the waiting taxicab. Bob asked, "Where do you go from here?"

"Home," said Father Mark.

"Where is home?" Bob asked.

"The Vatican," Father Mark replied.

Bob closed the door of the taxicab and the driver started the engine. The taxicab drove away.

Bob, Sally, Betty, and Sandra waved goodbye to Father Mark and Father Robert as the taxicab drove away.

Sally asked Bob, "Do you think all of this is true?"

Bob said, "No. If it was true it would be in the Bible."

Rachel Reveals Her Secret

Rachel stood in the hospital corridor. She had seen Laurie's mother and father leave Laurie's room with a doctor. Laurie's father had his arm around the shoulder of Laurie's mother. Laurie's mother was crying and the doctor spoke to them as they walked.

The three walked down the corridor toward the corner.

She waited until the three had turned the corner and she went into Laurie's room.

Rachel looked at Laurie. Laurie lay in the hospital bed and she was covered with bandages. Her face had many small cuts and there was a large cut on her forehead. The small cuts were stitched. Some of the small cuts had one stitch. Most of the cuts had three stitches.

The large cut on her forehead had many stitches. There were too many stitches to count.

Her eyes, nose, chin, and basically her whole head was bruised. The bruises were dark black.

There was a metal piece on her legs and one of her arms was in a plaster cast.

Laurie looked like she was asleep.

Rachel sat down in a chair near the bed.

Rachel and Laurie were alone in the hospital room.

Slowly, Laurie opened her eyes. She looked at Rachel.

"I'm pretty messed up," Laurie said.

When Laurie spoke, Rachel saw the dried blood in her mouth.

Rachel said, "You will get better."

"I do not know. I do not think so," Laurie said.

Laurie added, "I have not seen you in several weeks. I missed you."

"I missed you too," said Rachel.

"It all seems like a dream. One big, bad dream. I hope I will wake up and it's one big, bad dream. I'm scared. I'm really scared," said Laurie.

"Have you ever been sick Rachel? I mean really sick," asked Laurie.

Rachel said, "Yes. I was very sick when I was a baby."

"Have you been sick since?" asked Laurie.

"No," replied Rachel.

"Man, you must have a guardian angel or something," Laurie said.

"Or something," Rachel replied.

"Mom and dad left for a while. They will be back," Laurie said.

Rachel said, "I know. I saw them leave with the doctor. I can't stay long. When they return I will not be here."

"Where are your mom and dad?" Laurie asked.

"They are outside. They are waiting for me," Rachel said.

"Tell them to come in. I want to see them," said Laurie.

"They can't come in," added Rachel.

"Why not?" asked Laurie.

"Because I am going to tell you a secret. This is the biggest secret. My parents are not to hear what I am going to tell you," said Rachel.

"What kind of secret?" asked Laurie.

"The greatest secret," said Rachel.

"Why are you going to tell me this secret?" Laurie asked.

"Because we both play a part in it," said Rachel.

"Well! What is it?" asked Laurie.

Rachel said, "When I was an infant child, I was very sick. God sent a young boy to me and this young boy had a gift from God. This gift given to the boy from God was that God healed through his hands. God spoke to the boy in prayer."

"The boy touched me and God healed me through the hands of the boy. The gift God gave to the boy, God gave to me. God heals through my hands and God speaks to me in prayer."

"It is time for me to pass the gift from God to another."

"Am I the one God will give the gift to?" asked Laurie.

"No. God will give the gift to another. God has sent me to you. God will heal you through my hands and you will follow the will of God," Rachel said.

Laurie looked at her legs and she said, "I do not know. The doctors say I will never walk again. I have no feeling in my legs. My spine is broken."

"I know what the doctors said. The doctors are wrong," added Rachel.

Laurie was surprised. She asked, "How do you know about my legs? The doctor just told my mother and my father. That is why they are so upset. "

"God told me," said Rachel.

Rachel said, "The doctors only know what they know. They do not know of the will of God."

"How will God heal me?" asked Laurie.

"You will ask for God's blessing and you will touch my hand. I will touch you and God will heal you through my hands," said Rachel.

"When will God heal me?" asked Laurie.

"You will be healed in five days. Tomorrow, you will leave the hospital. Wednesday, your legs and your arm will move. Friday, you will be completely healed," said Rachel.

"Why will it take five days?" asked Laurie.

"Because the two of us need time to get away," said Rachel.

"Away? Where are you going?" asked Laurie.

"I can not tell you that," said Rachel.

"Why are you leaving?" asked Laurie.

"Because there are men who search for me. I must leave and travel far away," said Rachel.

"Have you done something wrong?" asked Laurie.

"No. I have done nothing wrong," said Rachel.

"Are these men bad or spies or something?" asked Laurie.

"No. These men are good men. These men follow God. They will not harm me," said Rachel.

"Why do these men search for you?" asked Laurie.

"They want to know what I know," said Rachel.

"What do you know?" asked Laurie.

"Everything," replied Rachel.

"Everything! Do you know who will win the Super Bowl?" asked Laurie.

"No. I do not know who will win the Super Bowl," said Rachel.

"Well, what do you know?" asked Laurie.

"I know of all the children to whom God has given this gift. The first child was named Rebecca. The second child was named Aaron. The third child was named Jessie. I know who the next child will be. I know of the children to come," said Rachel.

"Is that it?" asked Laurie.

"No. That is not it. One child prepares the way for the second coming," said Rachel.

"The second coming? You mean you know when Jesus Christ will return to earth?" asked Laurie.

"No. That is known only to God. I only know of the child," said Rachel.

Rachel said, "A young child will pass the gift to another. And God will perform great feats of healing through the hands of the child. And all will be made known of the child. And all will know of God's power through the hands of the child. And many will come unto God and the Christ through the child. And the child prepares the way for the second coming of Christ."

"And you know of this child?" asked Laurie.

"Yes. God revealed this to me. God revealed this to all the children to whom God gave the gift," said Rachel.

"Why do you tell me this?" asked Laurie.

"Because you are a part of God's plan. You will bring many unto God and Jesus. You will do God's will," said Rachel.

"What is it like? I mean, what is it like to follow God's will?" asked Laurie.

"You will know no fear or loneliness for God is with you. You will know peace, love, and great happiness," said Rachel.

"I have another secret," said Rachel.

"What is it?" asked Laurie.

"My real name is Elizabeth," said Rachel.

"Why did you change your name?" asked Laurie.

"Because it is not God's will that all men know of me. I have been given many names. I will be given many more. The one who comes after me will be known by many names," said Rachel.

"Will these men find you?" asked Laurie.

רבקה

"No. They will seek me and those who follow me. They will not find us for God does not will it so," said Rachel.

God Heals Laurie

"When will God heal me?" asked Laurie.

"Now!" said Rachel.

Laurie looked upward and she said, "I ask the blessing of God that I may do the will of God."

Laurie touched the hand of Rachel and Rachel touched the arm of Laurie.

Laurie felt a great peace come upon her. She felt a warm, gentle wave come upon her. All the pain left and Laurie could feel the cool sheet on her legs. She could feel the cold metal on her legs. Then, Laurie moved her right foot.

Laurie was no longer afraid for God was with her.

She began to cry. Laurie had never known such feelings.

Rachel said, "It is time for me to leave."

Laurie asked, "Will we see each other again?"

Rachel said, "Yes. Many years from now we will meet again."

Laurie began to giggle and she asked, "Will we be old ladies, eating crackers and drinking milk, living in an old folks home?"

Rachel said, "No. We will meet in the house of God."

Laurie quit laughing. She said, "I will tell no one of your secrets."

Rachel said, "I know. God told me you would keep my secrets."

Rachel went to the door and she opened the door.

Laurie asked, "One last question? When will God pass the gift to another?"

Rachel looked at her watch. "Fifteen minutes from now," she said.

The Gift is Passed to Another

The elevator sounded the ring for floor 6.

The door opened and three people emerged. They walked to the nurse's station and the man introduced himself as Eric. He introduced his wife Irene and their daughter Rachel. He asked to see Samuel.

The nurse stated that Samuel was in room 610. However, Samuel was very ill and he was not expected to survive. Samuel was born premature and his heart did not develop normally. The family was being allowed to be with him, as he was not expected to survive.

The nurse added that only a few visitors were allowed. They may not be allowed to stay very long.

Eric added, "We won't be long."

The three people walked to room 610. As they approached, the low cry of an infant could be heard. Eric slowly opened the door to see several people in the room. There was a man and a woman. There was a young girl and an infant. The woman held the infant. The child cried softly.

The man was the father of Samuel. The woman was Samuel's mother. The young girl was Samuel's older sister.

"Excuse us," Eric stated, "I am Eric. This is my wife Irene and our daughter Rachel. We were told that young Samuel was very ill."

The mother nodded her head.

Eric continued, "Our daughter was once very ill. God healed our daughter and God blessed our daughter. We are here to share that blessing."

The people in the room seemed perplexed. These people were unknown to them. They were strangers, yet their presence brought a peace and a calm.

Samuel's father motioned for them to enter.

Eric and Irene stood near the door. Their daughter Rachel sat on the floor before the mother and the child.

The child continued to cry. Samuel's mother said, " Our baby was born premature and his heart did not develop normally. He has many problems. The doctors have operated but there is little hope he will recover. The doctors believe he doesn't have much time to live."

"We have prayed to God for a miracle."

Rachel said, "God has heard your prayers and God has sent me to your son. God will heal your son through my hands and God will heal no other through my hands. For that which was given to me will be taken from me. And that which is taken from me will be given to your son. God will heal through the hands of your son."

The family looked at Rachel.

Rachel held out her arms and she spoke to Samuel's mother, "May I hold your son?"

Samuel's mother was reluctant to hand her son to the young girl. Her husband spoke softly, "Let her hold him."

Samuel's mother carefully placed Samuel in Rachel's arms. Samuel cried softly.

Rachel held the baby close and she whispered into his ear. The cries stopped.

Rachel looked at Samuel's mother and Samuel's father. She said, "The power of God has healed your son."

Rachel passed her hand over Samuel's head and body. She looked upward and whispered. She then looked at his mother and his father and said, "It is the will of God that generations to come will know the power of God through the hands of a child. What was given to me has been taken from me. What was taken from me has been given to your son."

Rachel again looked upward and she said, "Your son is protected by God himself. No man, woman, child, or beast of the earth shall harm your son. This is the will of God."

Rachel handed Samuel to his mother.

Rachel again spoke, "Your son Samuel will serve God. Return to your place and share the blessing which God has given."

רבקה

Appendix
The Children

Child's Name	Year C.E.	Gender / Race / Country
Rebecca	37	Girl/Hebrew
Aaron	44	Boy/Hebrew
Jessie	51	Boy/Hebrew
Hannah	58	Girl/Hebrew
Helsa	65	Girl/Hebrew
Semira	72	Girl/Hebrew
Avisha	79	Boy/Hebrew
Yahoash	86	Boy/Hebrew
Berakhiah	93	Boy/Hebrew
Jensine	100	Girl/Hebrew
Elhanan	107	Boy/Hebrew
Azaryahu	114	Boy/Hebrew
Manuela	121	Girl/Hebrew
Avidan	128	Boy/Hebrew
Elora	135	Girl/Hebrew
Abisha	142	Girl/Hebrew
Joachim	149	Boy/Hebrew
Zaneta	156	Girl/Hebrew
Raphael	163	Boy/Hebrew
Zedekiah	170	Boy/Hebrew
Hadar	177	Boy/Hebrew
Rafela	184	Girl/Hebrew
Taneli	191	Boy/Hebrew
Zadok	198	Boy/Hebrew
Aryeh	205	Boy/Hebrew
Malachy	212	Boy/Hebrew
Abiel	219	Boy/Hebrew
Beathag	226	Girl/Hebrew
Muslim	233	Boy/Egypt
Sadiki	240	Boy/Egypt
Halima	247	Girl/Egypt
Lateef	254	Boy/Egypt
Yahya	261	Boy/Egypt

רבקה

Child's Name	Year C.E.	Gender / Race / Country
Osahar	268	Boy/Egypt
Hakizimana	275	Boy/Egypt
Hasina	282	Girl/Egypt
Tumaini	289	Boy/Egypt
Eshe	296	Girl/Egypt
Yaminah	303	Girl/Egypt
Quibilah	310	Girl/Egypt
Chike	317	Boy/Egypt
Asim	324	Boy/Egypt
Nathifa	331	Girl/Egypt
Rashida	338	Girl/Egypt
Rashida	345	Girl/Egypt
Talibah	352	Girl/Egypt
Mandisa	359	Girl/Egypt
Jendayi	366	Girl/Egypt
Apophis	373	Boy/Egypt
Shani	380	Girl/Egypt
Agafia	387	Girl/Greece
Alena	394	Girl/Greece
Theon	401	Boy/Greece
Risto	408	Boy/Greece
Aretina	415	Girl/Greece
Cassie	422	Girl/Greece
Panteleimon	429	Boy/Greece
Lysander	436	Boy/Greece
Colette	443	Girl/Greece
Takis	450	Boy/Greece
Urian	457	Boy/Greece
Yalena	464	Girl/Greece
Theophilia	471	Girl/Greece
Habib	478	Boy/Africa
Iverem	485	Girl/Africa
Sisay	492	Girl/Africa
Basel	499	Boy/Africa
Akello	506	Boy/Africa
Abrihet	513	Girl/Africa
Iskinder	520	Boy/Africa

Child's Name	Year C.E.	Gender / Race / Country
Armani	527	Girl/Africa
Diara	534	Boy/Africa
Mariama	541	Girl/Africa
Chinaka	548	Girl/Africa
Adom	555	Boy/Africa
Jaja	562	Boy/Africa
Yohance	569	Boy/Africa
Uchechi	576	Boy/Africa
Uchenna	583	Girl/Africa
Zuwena	590	Girl/Africa
Berhanu	597	Boy/Africa
Desta	604	Boy/Africa
Anaya	611	Girl/Africa
Erasto	618	Boy/Africa
Tamirat	625	Boy/Africa
Sadio	632	Girl/Africa
Asabi	639	Girl/Africa
Amari	646	Boy/Africa
Ghedi	653	Boy/Africa
Amachi	660	Girl/Africa
Bab-EL-Sama	667	Girl/Arabia
Damaa	674	Girl/Arabia
Taleb	681	Boy/Arabia
Majeed	688	Boy/Arabia
Al-Hadiye	695	Boy/Arabia
Ferhan	702	Boy/Arabia
Yasmeen	709	Girl/Arabia
Mahfouz	716	Boy/Arabia
Pavaka	723	Boy/India
Agastya	730	Boy/India
Anasuya	737	Girl/India
Kailasa	744	Girl/India
Shakra	751	Girl/India
Deven	758	Boy/India
Kabir	765	Boy/India
Bhagwandas	772	Boy/India
Sevti	779	Girl/India

רבקה

Child's Name	Year C.E.	Gender / Race / Country
Sitara	786	Girl/India
Yasmine	793	Girl/India
Kirati	800	Girl/India
Fai	807	Boy/China
Liang	814	Boy/China
Na	821	Girl/China
An	827	Girl/China
Tao	834	Girl/China
Shen	841	Boy/China
Jun	848	Girl/China
Wei	855	Girl/China
Chen	862	Boy/China
Cong	869	Boy/China
Lian	876	Boy/China
Ping	883	Girl/China
Shaiming	890	Boy/China
Sying	897	Boy/China
Yan Yan	904	Girl/China
Yu Jie	911	Girl/China
Zhen	918	Girl/China
Long	925	Boy/China
Hoshiko	932	Boy/China
Li	939	Boy/China
Nyoko	946	Girl/Japan
Hiroshi	953	Boy/Japan
Shika	960	Girl/Japan
Yoshi	967	Boy/Japan
Kioko	974	Girl/Japan
Koto	981	Girl/Japan
Michio	988	Boy/Japan
Naoko	995	Girl/Japan
Renjiro	1002	Boy/Japan
Jomei	1009	Boy/Japan
Suki	1016	Girl/Japan
Yuki	1023	Boy/Japan
Kaede	1030	Girl/Japan
Kyoto	1037	Girl/Japan

Child's Name	Year C.E.	Gender / Race / Country
Chika	1044	Girl/Japan
Benjiro	1051	Boy/Japan
Kyoshi	1058	Boy/Japan
Kei	1065	Girl/Japan
Takeo	1072	Boy/Japan
Miya	1078	Girl/Japan
Shina	1085	Girl/Japan
Nami	1092	Girl/Japan
Sakura	1099	Girl/Japan
Kado	1106	Boy/Japan
Tamiko	1113	Girl/Japan
Dasha	1120	Girl/Russia
Yasha	1127	Boy/Russia
Fyodor	1134	Boy/Russia
Duscha	1141	Boy/Russia
Feodora	1148	Boy/Russia
Danya	1154	Boy/Russia
Semyon	1161	Boy/Russia
Ioakim	1168	Boy/Russia
Anna	1175	Boy/Russia
Vanya	1182	Girl/Russia
Elga	1189	Girl/Russia
Oleg	1196	Boy/Russia
Jelena	1203	Girl/Russia
Lubmilla	1210	Boy/Russia
Karina	1217	Boy/Russia
Staya	1224	Boy/Russia
Edik	1231	Boy/Russia
Yoana	1238	Girl/Spain
Alazne	1245	Girl/Spain
Amadeo	1252	Boy/Spain
Noe	1259	Boy/Spain
Mateo	1266	Boy/Spain
Benita	1273	Girl/Spain
Jose	1280	Boy/Spain
Casimiro	1287	Boy/Spain
Jesus	1294	Boy/Spain

רבקה

Child's Name	Year C.E.	Gender / Race / Country
Casta	1301	Girl/Spain
Sancia	1308	Girl/Spain
Raul	1315	Boy/Spain
Tobias	1322	Boy/Spain
Esperanza	1329	Girl/Spain
Helga	1336	Girl/Germany
Johanna	1343	Girl/Germany
Selik	1350	Boy/Germany
Oswald	1357	Boy/Germany
Wilhelm	1364	Boy/Germany
Engleberta	1371	Girl/Germany
Amara	1378	Girl/Germany
Maria	1385	Girl/England
Rebecca	1392	Girl/England
Victoria	1399	Girl/England
Eric	1406	Boy/England
Edward	1413	Boy/England
Raymond	1420	Boy/England
Ronald	1427	Boy/England
Annabelle	1434	Girl/England
Bruce	1441	Boy/England
Catherine	1448	Girl/England
Grace	1455	Girl/England
Michelle	1462	Girl/England
Valerie	1469	Girl/England
Elizabeth	1476	Girl/England
Ruth	1483	Girl/England
Michael	1490	Boy/England
Paul	1497	Boy/England
Rachel	1504	Girl/England
Samuel	1511	Boy/England
Winston	1518	Boy/England
Charles	1525	Boy/England
Harris	1532	Boy/England
Robert	1539	Boy/England
Suzanne	1546	Girl/England
Mary	1553	Girl/England

Child's Name	Year C.E.	Gender / Race / Country
Timothy	1560	Boy/England
Eirica	1567	Girl/Scotland
Leana	1574	Girl/Scotland
Tyra	1581	Girl/Scotland
Ronald	1588	Boy/Scotland
Bonnie	1595	Girl/Scotland
Macrae	1602	Boy/Scotland
Wallace	1609	Boy/Scotland
Carmichael	1616	Boy/Scotland
Christel	1623	Girl/Scotland
Isobel	1630	Girl/Scotland
Malcolm	1637	Boy/Scotland
Iain	1644	Boy/Scotland
Jean	1651	Girl/Scotland
Morrison	1658	Boy/Scotland
Parlan	1665	Boy/Scotland
Siubhan	1672	Girl/Scotland
Sinclair	1679	Boy/Scotland
Ailbert	1686	Boy/Scotland
Mackay	1693	Boy/Scotland
Brianna	1700	Girl/Ireland
Colmcilla	1707	Girl/Ireland
Fineena	1714	Girl/Ireland
Tullia	1721	Girl/Ireland
Seafraid	1728	Boy/Ireland
Malone	1735	Boy/Ireland
Terrence	1742	Boy/Ireland
Patrick	1749	Boy/Ireland
Aideen	1756	Girl/Ireland
Brian	1763	Boy/Ireland
Cristin	1770	Girl/Ireland
Eamon	1777	Boy/Ireland
Eveleen	1784	Girl/Ireland
Kathleen	1791	Girl/Ireland
Keegan	1798	Boy/Ireland
Moreen	1805	Girl/Ireland
Nolan	1812	Boy/Ireland

רבקה

Child's Name	Year C.E.	Gender / Race / Country
Quinlan	1819	Boy/Ireland
Whelan	1826	Boy/Ireland
Aengus	1833	Boy/Ireland
Eilis	1840	Girl/Ireland
Gilchrist	1847	Boy/Ireland
Godfrey	1854	Boy/Ireland
Jeoffroi	1861	Boy/France
Mahieu	1868	Boy/France
Esperanza	1875	Girl/France
Amedee	1882	Girl/France
Rene	1889	Boy/France
Elitta	1896	Girl/France
Sennet	1903	Boy/France
Cateline	1910	Girl/France
Benedetta	1917	Girl/Italy
Donato	1924	Boy/Italy
Matteo	1931	Boy/Italy
Agnella	1938	Girl/Italy
Giovanni	1945	Boy/Italy
Leonora	1952	Girl/Italy
Teodora	1959	Girl/Italy
Renata	1966	Girl/Italy
Maceo	1973	Boy/Italy
Amadeo	1980	Boy/Italy
Antonio	1987	Boy/Italy
Elizabeth	1994	Girl/America
Samuel *	2001	Boy/America

* Samuel was born in America. Samuel is of African decent.

The Author

Edward Ronny Arnold may have created the first electronic book. In 1984, he created a stand-alone computer program, which allowed a person to read the story in one of eight reading speeds. The story he created was titled, *The Story of Creation*. *The Story of Creation* is the computerized version of the first chapters of Genesis from the King James Version of the Holy Bible.

In 1989, Edward created the first electronic newspaper, *News Disk ®*. *News Disk ®* contained animation, real photographs, sound effects, and voice. The February 1990 issue, dedicated to Black History Month, included portions of a speech by Dr. Martin Luther King, Jr. The speech was the actual voice of Dr. Martin Luther King, Jr.

Edward's software programs have been nominated for several awards. Among the nominations are: *Number Cross™*, *Aesop's Fables - The Hare and the Tortoise*, and *News Disk ®*.

Rebecca © is Edward's first original novel. Edward holds the degrees of BS in Psychology and the MA in Sociology from Middle Tennessee State University. Edward resides in Nashville, Tennessee with his wife, Michelle, and their daughter, Khristine.

Rebecca © is published as an electronic book on the **Computer Classics ®** website. You have purchased the paperback version of the electronic book.

Rebecca © is a book, which will be read for many years.

רבקה

Upcoming Books

Fall 2002

The Lepers – A prequel to *Rebecca*. The lepers journeyed to Jerusalem to see the Great Healer. But who was the Great Healer? The Great Healer was Jesus Christ. The lepers traveled to Jerusalem to welcome Jesus into the city. When they arrive, Jesus had been crucified and buried. The lepers refused to leave. This is a powerful story of the faith of the outcast. This book covers the birth of Rebecca and how she contracted leprosy.

Spring 2003

Rashida – God took the gift from Rashida and gave the gift to an unnamed child. The unnamed child is given the name of Rashida. Rashida looks like the deceased daughter of an Egyptian soldier. The Egyptian soldier befriends Rashida and her adoptive family. A touching story of the soldier who befriends the family.

Fall 2003

Habib – A Greek ship comes into port to be greeted by a young girl named Theophilia. God has sent Theophilia to a young boy on the ship named Habib. Who is Habib? The ship's hold is full of Africans, taken by force, to be sold as slaves. This is an exciting story of God's love for all mankind. God sends the angel Jaykal to return the captured people to their home.

Spring 2004

The Tenth Scroll – The book everyone is waiting for. Who wrote the tenth scroll? What does it say? Why did Titus not reveal the scroll? All of your questions will be answered. *The Tenth Scroll* has already been written. It is scheduled for release in the spring of 2004.

Spring 2008

Samuel – In the year 2001, God took the gift from Elizabeth and gave the gift to Samuel. In the year 2008, Samuel will pass the gift to another. Who is Samuel? What has happened in Samuel's life? The story of Samuel does not begin in the year 2001. The story of Samuel begins in the year 478. Descendents of Samuel are captured in Africa and taken to Greece to be sold as slaves. God sends the angel Jaykal to return the captured people to their home. This is an exciting book that traces the descendents of

Samuel from the continent of Africa to the Civil Rights movement in the 1960's. Samuel is descended from Habib.

No Date Given

El-Mabka – the Place of Weeping – "A young child will pass the gift to another. And God will perform great feats of healing through the hands of the child. And all will be made known of the child. And all will know of God's power through the hands of the child. And many will come unto God and the Christ through the child." This is the final book related to *Rebecca. El-Mabka – the Place of Weeping* has already been written. No date of publication has been given.